ESCAPE FROM HAT

ADAM KLINE AND BRIAN TAYLOR

ESCAPE FROM HAT

HARPER
An Imprint of HarperCollinsPublishers

Library of Congress Control Number: 2019944052

ISBN 978-0-06-283997-8

Typography by Andrea Vandergrift

19 20 21 22 23   SCP   10 9 8 7 6 5 4 3 2 1

❖

First Edition

Originally published in 2012 by ZOVA Books

For the boy who had only bad luck
and the black cat who chose to be good.

CHAPTER ONE

Cecil Bean had both good luck and bad.

Once a little girl had thrown a big wet wad of watermelon chewing gum from the balcony of her fourth-floor flat, and it had landed in Cecil's hair—a particularly unpleasant circumstance, given that Cecil was mildly allergic to watermelon. And when Cecil sneezed, he sneezed so hard that fallen leaves and scraps of trash flew wildly about, an especially large section of the village newspaper sticking directly to the side of his noggin.

But just out of the corner of his eye, Cecil could see that the proprietor of the Fancy Lad Barbershop had placed a large advertisement in the newspaper. In honor of the salon's sesquicentennial anniversary, all little boys named Cecil would receive a complimentary haircut, courtesy of their finest coiffeur. When Cecil emerged from the shop, freshly coiffed, the chewing-gum thrower glanced down from the balcony of her fourth-floor flat and promptly decided that boys were substantially more interesting than she had previously thought.

"Hey, little boy!" she cried down to Cecil. "I like the cut of your jib!"

That was the sort of luck that Cecil had. Something terrible would happen, and then something quite pleasant would inevitably follow. But as to precisely *why* he experienced such extremes of luck, Cecil had no idea. Most people don't.

The bad luck was Millikin's fault.

You see, every person in the entire world is stalked by his or her very own personal black cat. And Millikin was Cecil's. Millikin's assignment was to cross Cecil's path as often as he could possibly manage it. Because every time he did, something bad would happen to Cecil. Sometimes the bad things would be relatively minor, like misplacing the key to his bicycle lock, and sometimes they'd be a bit more serious, like accidentally putting chili peppers on his peanut butter sandwich.

Black cats don't come from our world. They come from a dark and shadowy realm and only enter ours during working hours, to busy themselves crossing our paths and making mischief. Millikin liked his job. He did not, on the other hand, like Leek.

Leek followed Cecil everywhere, because Leek was Cecil's personal lucky rabbit. (Everyone has one, of course, but we almost never notice them because they're so exceptionally clever.) Each time some calamity would befall Cecil Bean, Leek would brush against the hem of his trousers, and everything would instantly be just dandy—or even better than dandy, as in the case of the aforementioned chewing gum incident.

Leek was the seven-hundred-and-seventy-seventh son of a seven-hundred-and-seventy-seventh son, which made him an especially magical lucky rabbit. But Leek didn't come from some mysterious and shadowy realm like Millikin did. Leek came from the garden behind the Bean cottage, where he lived in a cozy hole just left of the bok choy.

Like Millikin, Leek loved his job. Unlike Millikin, he also loved Cecil Bean—with every single fiber of his being. If it had been left entirely up to Leek, which it wasn't, Cecil wouldn't have had any bad luck at all. But given the long-standing conflict between the black cats and lucky rabbits, Leek simply had no choice but to keep one watchful eye on Cecil and the other on Millikin.

"Millikin," Leek would say to himself, "is a rapscallion." (Which is a five-dollar word for *scoundrel*. If Leek had known any ten-dollar words for *scoundrel*, he would have used one of those, too.)

Millikin, on the other hand, had endured just about all the interference from Leek he cared to endure. It was all so terrifically frustrating! When Millikin engineered a thunderstorm to soak Cecil down to his tighty-whities, Leek conjured up a bright yellow rain slicker, with matching boots to boot. When the cat summoned a legion of chicken pox to ruin Cecil's holiday vacation, Leek answered with a rare strain of immunoglobulin known as *Vulpes carnivorous*, which promptly ate the chicken pox whole. And when Millikin somehow managed to surround the Bean residence in a ring of steaming green dog poop, so that Cecil would be sure to step in multiple piles, Leek produced a tribe of dung beetles, who rolled the poop away in tidy little balls and played bocce.

After a veritable lifetime of defeat, Millikin had endured quite enough, in large part because it made him so deeply unhappy. Millikin had spoken at length with his therapist, who concluded quite logically that Leek was the root of the problem. For with every crushing loss, Millikin's confidence waned, his self-worth contracted, and all that remained was a nagging sense of *ennui*, which is a five-dollar word for depression. It was all Leek's fault, his therapist had announced. Millikin would never ever know true joy so long as that meddlesome magic rabbit was foiling all his plans.

That's when Millikin had The Most Sinister Idea of His Life™.

What would happen, wondered Millikin, if he were to cross Leek's path rather than Cecil's?

Now it was just about this time that a very curious sort of caravan emerged from the Northern Wilds and clickety-clacked its way rather ominously toward the center of town. Unlike a proper caravan, this caravan wasn't crimson red and sparkly gold, filled with acrobats and paper hats and soda pop freezing cold. No, this caravan was dusty and crusty and hauled by a feeble affair, a rickety rickshaw built on the cheap with parts from a Chevy Corvair. All this caravan contained were a few shoddy parlor tricks and one conniving old man, who called himself a magician. His name was the Great Imbrolio, and on his head, he wore a tall black hat that didn't really belong to him but was, at the time, in his possession.

The following morning, Leek emerged from his hole in the garden and readied himself for work. Cecil was just departing the little Bean cottage, and Leek decided that, if he could manage it, the boy would have an exceptionally lucky day—possibly something involving chocolate eclairs. The magic rabbit thusly hopped off to follow Cecil as he set about his errands.

What Leek had failed to notice was that just ahead of him, a dark and shadowy feline form had snuck across his path, forming an invisible line of ill luck—which Leek unwittingly stepped across.

Precisely six seconds later, Leek saw The Turnip.

It was just sitting there, big as you please, smelling for all the world like the most delectable turnip that ever was. As the turnip's savory bouquet wafted invitingly in Leek's direction, his whiskers twitched, and his stomach growled rather crudely.

"It would be a disservice to Cecil," reasoned Leek, "were I not to fortify myself with this turnip."

But when Leek hoisted the turnip, which truly was a specimen of the very highest quality, everything went black. The turnip, you see, was more than just a turnip. It was bait.

Needless to say, the day did not go even mildly well for Cecil. The boy couldn't remember a more unlucky day in his life! Millikin considered it a great victory that when Cecil arrived home that evening, his knees were scraped, his toes were stubbed, and his marbles were all quite lost, through holes in each of his pockets. Positively reeking from a chance encounter with an unreasonably territorial skunk, poor Cecil Bean had even contracted a rare breed of poison ivy that, for whatever reason, affects only one's bottom.

The only thing that might possibly have salvaged

Cecil's day was The Magic Show.

All the village children were abuzz with excitement, and as dusk settled forebodingly over the town, a sizable crowd assembled around the mysterious caravan of the Great Imbrolio, who emerged from within in a burst of purple smoke.

"My name," said the Great Imbrolio, "is the Great Imbrolio. And I am a famous magician."

"Huzzah!" bellowed the crowd.

"Huzzah!" cried Cecil, absently scratching his bottom.

"And now," hissed the Great Imbrolio, "on with the show!"

Sadly, Imbrolio's show was anything but magical. His deck of cards was clearly stacked. His Mystical Orb of Levitation quite obviously dangled from twine. And the length of colorful scarves he withdrew from his fist was plainly stuffed down a pant leg. Long before the Great Imbrolio had even approached his best material, the crowd began to protest.

"Fraud!"

"Charlatan!"

"Swindler!"

"Cheat!"

"Goober!"

It was painfully clear to all assembled that Imbrolio wasn't great by any stretch of the imagination whatsoever. What no one could possibly have known, at least not yet, was that they *were* in the presence of something truly special, of wonder and deep magic. For while Imbrolio himself was decidedly ordinary— and well below average with regard to personal hygiene—he did have something quite extraordinary up his sleeve. Or rather, on his head.

"Silence!"

Something in Imbrolio's voice was so horrific, so chilling, that even the muscular guy in back figured he'd better stop flexing his pecs and calling people "goober."

"For my final trick, I will require a volunteer from the audience."

Cecil Bean raised the hand that wasn't busy scratching his behind.

"You there, boy! Step forward!"

Which Cecil did. And when he did, the Great Imbrolio handed him his hat.

"Would you say, boy, that this hat is an absolutely normal hat? Would you say that you have never inspected a more normal hat in all your life?"

Cecil inspected the hat. It was tall and black, with a bright red lining. But aside from smelling a bit like the Great Imbrolio, it certainly seemed quite normal. So Cecil nodded, acknowledging the hat's apparent normalcy.

"And would you say, dear boy, that THIS is a normal rabbit?"

The Great Imbrolio reached beneath the folds of his cloak and withdrew a rabbit, holding him by the ears.

It was Leek.

Cecil looked at Leek, and Leek looked at Cecil. Cecil felt that the rabbit's eyes were tinged with a great sadness, and he couldn't quite shake the feeling that the rabbit seemed somehow familiar. But Cecil could not deny that otherwise, it seemed just as normal as the hat.

"Quite right," said the magician. "And now, citizens of this pathetic little backwater, behold the greatness of Imbrolio! Behold as I utter ancient incantations in the long-forgotten tongue of the mystics! Behold, be amazed"—this last part, the old man whispered only to Leek—"and *beware*."

The Great Imbrolio thrust Leek into the hat. When Cecil peered inside a mere half moment later, the rabbit was gone.

The crowd gasped in amazement. Now *that* was a magic trick.

Cecil waited patiently as the magician bowed and waved and strutted about triumphantly. But patience is a virtue only some of the time, and as far as Cecil was concerned, this wasn't one of those times. So he tugged on a corner of the great magician's cloak.

"When are you going to bring him back?" asked Cecil.

The Great Imbrolio's eyes narrowed, and he stared down at Cecil the same way one stares at the hindquarters of a big hairy worm after biting its fore-quarters from an apple.

"The show," he declared, "is over."

And with that, the caravan rolled promptly from town. You see, Imbrolio did not choose to admit that, in fact, he hadn't the faintest idea how to bring any-thing back from within the hat, let alone Leek. What's more, and as you'll soon discover, the hat wasn't even *his*.

Leek screamed as he fell. He fell for so long that eventually he had to take a very deep breath and start screaming all over again. But eventually, Leek peered down at a large patch of whiteness, which grew steadily larger. Then, rather faster than he'd expected, Leek plunged headlong into the whiteness, which as it turns out was snow.

Leek sat for a moment and gazed about, shaking the snow from his whiskers. All around him, in every direction as far as the eye could see, was snow. He had fallen into an endless tundra of perfect solitude, with the exception of a single black dot that seemed to be moving very slowly along the horizon. Leek stared at the dot and thought about Cecil, considering all the terrible twists of fate now certain to come his way, and really wished he hadn't bothered with that turnip.

Then the dot stopped, and Leek had the distinct impression that it was watching him. Which it was.

Precisely six seconds later, the dot was standing before him. But now that it was so close, it was hardly a dot anymore. It clearly was a monster.

The monster stood over Leek, belching steam from a variety of orifices. Then a hole opened in the center of the monster's head, and a black cat peeked out.

"Interloper!" cried the cat. (Which is a five-dollar word for someone who's somewhere he's not supposed to be.)

The monster with the cat in its head raised a hoof altogether larger, Leek thought, than the entire Bean cottage. And Leek froze, which is something rabbits do when they're so frightened that the blood runs cold in their veins, a state that renders an otherwise nimble creature about as fast as the average ice cube.

But as the hoof hurtled toward him, Leek felt a strong tug from beneath the snow. And altogether unexpectedly, the rabbit found himself pulled down, down through the snow, into a low tunnel, which shuddered violently as the monstrous hoof struck the ice pack above.

Standing before Leek was a she-rabbit, who whispered, "The surface isn't safe to walk alone. The Dimmer-Dammers are always watching."

"I'm sorry," said Leek, "but I'm afraid I've lost my way. I'm responsible for a little boy named Cecil Bean, who lives in a cottage on a hill. I myself live in the Bean family garden, in a cozy hole just left of the bok choy. And it's absolutely imperative that I return to my boy at once. I can't imagine what awful luck he must be having without me there to save the day!"

"We've all lost our humans," said the she-rabbit, turning into the darkness and beckoning Leek to follow.

Then she paused and glanced back, staring at Leek with a stare that made his whiskers twitch.

"My name is Morel," said the she-rabbit. "Welcome to Hat."

Just then, Cecil Bean, far away in an utterly separate world, stepped in an enormous pile of steaming green dog poop. Yes, his luck had turned for the worse.

CHAPTER
TWO

Leek followed Morel through a series of catacombs carved in the ancient ice. It was so cold that Leek could see his breath! Tiny icicles even formed at the tips of his whiskers—a circumstance that never occurred in his cozy little hole in the garden.

Before long, the tunnels came to an end, emerging in a great cavern of sapphire ice that sparkled with golden torchlight. The cavern, much to Leek's surprise, was filled with hundreds of rabbits, who turned their heads to gaze at him with curiosity. Leek gazed shyly back and stuck close to Morel, who led him to a crude chair in which sat a very old rabbit indeed.

"Old one," said Morel, bowing her head with respect, "yet another has fallen from the sky."

The elder raised his dark black eyes to stare at Leek, and Leek had the distinct impression he was being inspected both outside and in. Then the elder rabbit sighed, deeply and sadly, and spoke.

"I am Komatsuna," said he. "The first to come to Hat. Many moons have passed since I was seized by the nefarious Imbrolio, and many more have waxed and waned as my clan has grown. Here, beneath the ice, we seek refuge from the Dimmer-Dammers, and wait, without hope, for salvation. I bid you welcome."

"Thank you very much," squeaked Leek, "but I'm afraid I'm unable to stay. You see, I am in charge of a little boy named Cecil Bean, and I simply must return to him at once."

"It is impossible," replied Komatsuna. "There is no return from Hat. You, and your human Bean, are doomed."

Leek didn't much like the sound of that and turned to stare in wonder at Komatsuna's clan.

"But there are hundreds of you! Do you mean to

say that you've all abandoned your humans? Think of the terrible luck they must be having!"

"Not all have lost their wards," said Komatsuna. "Only a fraction of us ever lived among the humans, though we have since multiplied."

"O . . . kay," said Leek, trying valiantly to grasp the situation. "But there's got to be *some* way back," he considered. "There's always a way, with luck!"

Morel watched Komatsuna closely, wondering if he would dare to speak of The Only Way There Was. The sad old rabbit closed his sad black eyes in deep and somber thought.

"It is said there is a way," spoke Komatsuna, in a whisper. "A way that lies across the Great Ink. Far beyond the Jungle Prime Evil, through the Grottos of Ill Repute. For there, far beyond the reach of luck, lies the fortress of the black cats. There, in a barren land bereft of leaf or root, it is said there is a way."

"Well, that doesn't sound so bad," said Leek, his ears twitching optimistically.

"There, at the very heart of that luck-forsaken citadel, is a tower. And within, it is said that a rabbit may return to its human, through *magic*. But many have sought the tower, and none has ever reached it."

"I will reach it," said Leek. "I must. For Cecil Bean."

"And how will you reach it, young one, without luck?" inquired Komatsuna. "For luck is a gift that must be given. No rabbit can provide its own."

"I will go with Leek and be his guide," said Morel, surprising all assembled—including herself. "Long have I hidden from the Dimmer-Dammers, with great fear and loathing. But I too miss my human. And for her, I will brave the perils of Hat. For her, I will join this Leek, and we will give each other luck. Hear me, old one. I have spoken."

Komatsuna bowed his hoary head and stroked his ashen mustache. He had learned many things, both in our world and in Hat, and foremost among them was the fact that he had never won an argument with Morel, who was unusually brave and equally stubborn and typically heavily armed. Crossing Morel was risky business. So Komatsuna sighed and acquiesced.

"If such is your decision," he said at length, "you had better take a good supply of neeps."

After a long and successful day of crossing Cecil's path and causing all manner of calamities, Millikin returned to Hat. It had been a most refreshing feeling to note that whatever wrong he caused, Leek never once appeared to set things right. Millikin wished he had crossed Leek's path sooner, in which case he would probably already be happy. But at least now he was finally well on his way. In fact, thanks to Millikin, Cecil had caught a bad cold and been sent promptly to bed, only to find it infested with bedbugs, which were most certainly biting. Success.

Deep within the fortress of the black cats, Millikin was bragging to his friends over a bit of catnip, which for once he'd decisively earned. And oh, how his wicked brethren purred with approval! But just when he was getting to the best part, a feline scout strode into the room and posted a picture on the bulletin board.

"New rabbit," he said. "I spotted him in Sector Thirteen."

Millikin couldn't believe his eyes. For there, staring back at him from the bulletin board, was Leek.

Now, some black cats would have been quite content to know that their archnemeses had been banished to a dark and shadowy realm from which no hapless rabbit had ever returned. But Millikin was, as you know, an especially desperate black cat. And what's more, he knew all too well that Leek was an especially persistent lucky rabbit. This did not bode well.

Of all the places he might have ended up, thought Millikin, it just had to be here. This will not stand!

"Allocate all available resources to the capture of this rabbit," hissed Millikin aloud. "Dispatch the Dimmer-Dammers immediately, and engage with extreme prejudice. Sharpen your claws, army of darkness. For if I know Leek—and believe me, I do—he's headed directly for us—and for Cecil Bean."

Cecil Bean lay bedridden for several days, sniffling and sneezing and coughing and wheezing—and all the while trying desperately to fend off the battalion of bedbugs that had somehow appeared in his bed. At first, Cecil had assumed that a little bird or perhaps some exotic breed of anteater would happen along to dispatch the bedbugs. Perhaps a shriveled old woman would appear at his cottage door, bearing some fragrant poultice that would instantly cure his cold. But no such luck. It was the strangest thing. Cecil had experienced all sorts of bad luck over the years, but in the past, good luck had always made things better. Now, all of a sudden, his good luck seemed to have just . . . disappeared.

After several miserable days and nights, Cecil felt just well enough to get up, much to the disappointment of the bedbugs. And though the boy felt grave uncertainty about stepping out of doors, where all manner of ill luck undoubtedly awaited, he did have a hankering for a hot scone bathed in butter and apricot preserves. It didn't seem like much to ask.

So Cecil walked the little gravel path to the village, all the while watching very carefully for dark clouds, mud puddles, rabid dogs, and plagues of locusts—anything that might ruin his day. And soon enough, without noteworthy mishap, he came to his favorite café, widely renowned for its scones, which were baked fresh very early every morning of the week.

"I would like one hot scone, please," said Cecil to the restaurateur, "with butter and apricot preserves."

"We're out of scones," replied the restaurateur, "as well as butter and preserves. All we have left is liver. And I'm afraid it isn't overly fresh."

Cecil paused a moment before walking right back out to sit on the curb and cry. Cecil didn't care for liver of even the freshest variety. He didn't much like to cry, either, but it did happen on rare occasions when it seemed that all was surely lost and that he'd never be happy again. This was one of those times—and perhaps the worst time that Cecil could ever remember.

"It seems that someone," said a voice from behind him, "is down on his luck."

Cecil turned to spy a mysterious gentleman sitting at a small table, aglow in a narrow but brilliant swath of sunshine. The gentleman was having breakfast, and he had been watching Cecil for some time. As he looked upon the boy seated sadly on the curb, a passing motorcar whizzed through a deep puddle, soaking Cecil right down to his tighty-whities.

"Join me for breakfast?" offered the mysterious gentleman. "I happen to have an extra scone."

Cecil sadly sloshed over and sat down. The proffered scone was, surprisingly, still steaming. What's more, there was even a bit of butter as well as apricot preserves.

"Thank you very much," said Cecil.

"You're quite welcome," replied the gentleman. "It seems the least one can do for a boy who's lost his lucky rabbit."

Cecil didn't quite know what to make of that.

"Oh yes, it's all too obvious," said the gentleman, noting the boy's confusion. "You are lacking in luck, a circumstance that indicates the absence of your rabbit. And without said rabbit, you haven't anyone to offset the devious machinations of your personal black cat. Quite the tragic affliction. I've seen it before."

Cecil wondered if the mysterious gentleman was just slightly off his rocker. But the sparkle in his eye seemed more sincere than mad.

"Everyone in the world experiences good luck and bad, courtesy of the rabbits and cats, respectively," explained the gentleman. "One almost never sees them, of course, but there are many simple truths in the world that one never actually sees. Black cats are terribly clever creatures, with very few natural predators, so one rarely loses one's cat. But lucky rabbits are a different matter. The rabbits do have predators— and one especially bad one in particular. I wonder if perhaps you've heard of a man named Imbrolio."

"The magician!" cried Cecil.

"Hardly," huffed the gentleman, rolling his eyes. "The Great Imbrolio is neither great nor is he a true magician. But he does possess one item of true magic, an item I suspect we may blame for the disappearance of your rabbit."

"The hat!" said Cecil. Suddenly the boy realized why the sad little rabbit from Imbrolio's trick had seemed so exceedingly familiar: he'd known him, in a way, all his life.

"But how do you know all this?" he asked the mysterious gentleman.

"Because it's my hat."

"Oh," replied Cecil, for lack of a better reply.

"At least it was," said the gentleman with a sigh. "You see, Imbrolio was once my assistant. Not a very good one, of course. No panache, you see, and no respect for true magic whatsoever. One day, I awoke to find that he'd stolen away and taken my hat with him. But I suppose I might have expected as much from a fellow with no panache."

"What a terrible stroke of bad luck!" exclaimed Cecil.

"Luck? Not at all, my boy. Really more a matter of poor manners. Good and bad luck hold little sway over me, you see. My own lucky rabbit currently resides in a retirement community, pursuing a long-standing interest in model trains, of all things. We're still in touch at holidays. And my cat quit ages ago, once he realized that his powers were utterly ineffectual."

"But how can that be?" wondered Cecil. "Everyone has good and bad luck."

"Indeed," replied the gentleman. "But I know something that very few people know."

"What's that?"

"A true magician," said the gentleman, "never reveals his secrets."

"Oh," replied Cecil, again for lack of a better reply.

"But I will reveal this." The gentleman smiled kindly. "A rabbit can, in fact, be extracted from my hat. Imbrolio just doesn't know how. So should you decide that your rabbit is in need of saving, you need only find the hat and extract him. It's a surprisingly simple process, should one know the magic word."

"What's the magic word?" inquired Cecil, deciding right there and then that extraction of his lucky rabbit was of paramount import.

"As I said, a true magician never reveals his

secrets. Against our code, you see. But the answers to even the greatest of secrets are often right before us, if we only choose to look."

Cecil considered the mysterious gentleman's cryptic words, which were far too cryptic for his taste. But the man *had* given him a scone, which was something. And Cecil knew there was little use in asking a true magician to break the magician's code. So he rose to his feet, and what little chest he had swelled in staunch resolution.

"Then I must find the villain Imbrolio," said Cecil, "and save my rabbit. Thank you for the scone."

With that, off dashed Cecil Bean, in search of the magic hat. As he ran, the mysterious gentleman sipped his tea and watched, and whispered a final farewell.

"Good luck."

CHAPTER THREE

"**N**eeps," said Morel.

Leek and Morel had been walking for some time, long enough for Leek to realize that in Hat, the sun never shines. This, of course, means that very little grows in Hat. There are no parsnips, no fresh herbs, and certainly no green beans. What do grow are horrid, nasty things fueled by moonlight: black trees covered in thorns and sticky, creeping vines. Still, the rabbits had found that within their icy refuge it was possible to raise a rather bitter brand of rutabaga, which didn't taste particularly pleasant but was certainly better than nothing. This rutabaga, once properly cured and dried, made for a passable means of sustenance, quite filling even in small amounts—and perfect for long adventures. Morel carried a small pouch of the stuff, which the pair had stopped to nibble.

"Neeps are what we call it once it's dried."

Leek munched sadly on his share, thinking all the while of his garden and his boy.

"We should keep moving," said Morel. With that, she hoisted her weapons: a sharp sword slung at her back and a long spear, which she held before her in a most intimidating fashion. Leek himself carried no weapons. He had never felt the need for such things back home, and he had absolutely no idea how to use a conventional blade, as Morel clearly did. Leek had always felt that luck was his most potent weapon, though it was somehow reassuring to see Morel so heavily armed. Morel gave Leek a number of pleasant feelings, and reassurance was one of them.

"Stop daydreaming and hop to it," snapped Morel, "or a Dimmer-Dammer will get you."

Leek followed obediently, hopping after Morel

just as quickly as he could. Leek caught up with his guide at the crest of a low rise, where the pair was met by a frigid gust of wind and a sight that made Leek's whiskers curl with dread. For there before them, stretching gigantic and abysmal as far as the eye could see, was an ocean of pure and bottomless black.

"Behold the Great Ink," whispered Morel. "Treacherous, bottomless, and dank. To brave its crossing means certain death for most."

"But I must cross it," said Leek, "for my boy."

Morel did not respond but instead set about constructing a crude raft. She quickly felled a dozen thorny trees and stripped them of their vines, which snarled at the bite of her blade. In such a way, Morel soon lashed together the tiny vessel she hoped would carry them across. Leek, whom Morel regarded as largely useless, attempted to straighten his whiskers. He didn't want Morel to know he was afraid.

"Help me push it into the surf," she said.

Together, the rabbits pushed their craft into the blackness and hopped aboard. As it slipped slowly away from shore, Leek glanced back and wondered if it might not be so bad to live in an icy cave for the rest of his life, where he'd be chilly but categorically safe. But not Morel, who didn't once look back. Morel looked only forward, for she too had a human to consider. Before long, the shoreline behind them faded into the Great Ink forever, and Leek caught himself hoping the same wouldn't happen to them.

"How long will it take to cross?" asked Leek, rather fearing Morel's response.

"I cannot say. Few have dared to brave the Ink, and none has ever returned. There are tales of that which lies beyond, but I do not trust my fate to tales. I trust only my spear."

"Well, it is a very nice spear," said Leek awkwardly. It was strange that, although covered entirely in a cozy suit of thick brown fur, Leek felt rather exposed around Morel. Which is to say, the she-rabbit made Leek starkly aware of all his flaws and fears, in a way he'd never been before. And yet she also made him feel as if he might prove awfully brave in a pinch. It was very strange indeed, feeling so flawed yet filled with potential. And Leek wasn't quite certain what such strange feelings might come to mean in the end.

The pair sailed on in silence, a silence so profound that Leek finally decided to whistle a bit, just to be sure his ears were still working.

Then came a very faint sound, a deep drone that gave Leek's ears very grave misgivings.

"I hear something!" whispered Leek.

Morel had heard it, too. She scanned the horizon, her warrior's eyes and ears on full alert, trying to pinpoint its source.

"It's all around us," she realized, her voice grim with dread. And then she saw them.

"Dimmer-Dammers."

From every direction came the Dimmer-Dammers: iron ships propelled at great speed by engines of mammoth size and power. Each emblazoned with the telltale logo of doom, the ships exhaled vapors that stank of sheer contempt. "We are lost," Morel whispered to herself, "before we have scarcely begun."

Leek could only watch as the ring of Dimmer-Dammers grew tight as a nautical noose. But before it closed upon them, the mighty dreadnoughts slowed and came to a halt. And to Leek's everlasting surprise, an all-too-familiar black cat strode forward from the maw of his dark vessel and grinned, exposing his hideous fangs.

"Millikin!"

"I'd thought myself rid of you for good," sneered the cat. "Yet here you are, out for a cruise in my pool. And with a girlfriend no less!"

"I am his guide and no more," snapped Morel, brandishing her spear. "There are many ways to skin a cat, as I will gladly show you."

"Alas, I haven't time." Millikin yawned. "You see, I've a little boy named Cecil Bean to think about, and I've been dreaming up all sorts of wicked things to do to him. Action item number one involves a large dog with a very full bladder and the tree where Cecil likes to sit and read."

"Feckless hooligan!" cried Leek.

"But first," said the cat with a smile, "I will see you sink to the depths of the darkest void."

Before she quite knew what was happening, Morel found that she had stepped in front of Leek, as if to shield him from the danger. For a moment, she wondered why. But Morel would do the same for any rabbit, she supposed, even one as useless as Leek. Wouldn't she?

As the she-rabbit stood before him, Leek also instinctively feared for his companion. But to fight was not his way. Instead, Leek reached gently for Morel and lightly brushed her coat with a paw—just as he would normally brush against the hem of Cecil's trousers.

"Dimmer-Dammers," cried Millikin, "ready torpedoes, and fire at will!"

But before the torpedoes could be willfully fired, the black murk beneath the raft grew just slightly blacker, then started to churn and boil. Millikin's eyes narrowed to mere slits; he wasn't quite sure what was happening.

That's when a monster burst from the depths, mouth agape, to swallow the rabbits whole, raft and all.

The leviathan's great bulk, encrusted with stones and mollusks, soared into the sky, eclipsing—for a moment—the moon. Its jaws snapped shut with a sinister, slimy slap, and with that, it twisted and plunged, back into the icy depths, soaking the cats in the process.

Millikin shivered, shook the water from his back, and thoughtfully licked one wet paw with his venomous, sandpaper tongue.

"Bad luck for you, old foe," he snarled, "and good riddance."

Leek thought it had been dark before, but the darkness inside the fish was something altogether different. There, deep within the bowels of the monster, even the cold moon of Hat could never reach. Leek couldn't see the familiar tips of his whiskers, let alone Morel. He wished very hard for a carrot, as carrot consumption helps one to see in the dark. But alas, carrots simply don't grow deep within the bowels of sea monsters. That's a fact.

Morel, however, was a resourceful type of she-rabbit, and Leek could hear her rustling and bustling about. Soon enough, she had located the remains of their raft, and hacked a section of thorny wood from a log. She then struck a bit of tinder, still dry in its little waxed pouch, and produced a torch.

"That's better," said Morel.

But things weren't really better, she thought. They had escaped the insidious Dimmer-Dammers only to be swallowed whole by a fish. No, she thought, things weren't really better at all.

"At least we're together." Leek smiled.

Morel could only roll her eyes. She was quite accustomed to fighting and surviving all by herself and even liked it that way. At present, you see, Morel found little value in togetherness.

Then came the faintest sound of music. It was a sad and lonely sound, to be sure, but that didn't make it any less surprising.

"What's that?" whispered Leek.

"Only courage can answer such questions," snapped Morel, clutching her spear before her. And with that, she strode forward, ever deeper into the gullet of the fish. Leek felt rather short on courage at the moment, but of course he quickly followed. To Leek, togetherness seemed increasingly important.

Leek went with Morel through the innards of the fish, and as they crept along, the music grew somewhat louder. When they reached the entrance to the monster's cavernous stomach, Morel peeked in and beheld an unexpected sight.

In the far corner of the stomach was a shack, constructed of trash and bone and all manner of undigested detritus. From within came the unmistakable glow of a hearth, which Morel could not deny seemed faintly cozy. And sitting on the stoop of the shack, dolefully playing a miniature flute, was . . .

"A mouse!"

Leek had summoned just enough courage to peep over Morel's shoulder, and he had cried out prior to thinking twice. Leek wasn't stealthy like Morel.

The mouse looked up in pure and utter shock, dropping his flute midnote.

"They've found me!" he gasped. "At last, my doom has come!"

But before he could scurry into his shack and bar its feeble door, Morel strode forward, holding her torch aloft.

"It is not doom that seeks you here this day," she said. "We are simply two rabbits, wayfarers of the savage lands, and we are doomed ourselves."

The mouse's eyes grew wide in wonder and relief, and his muzzle ceased to quiver quite so much.

"Brown coats and long ears!" he said. "Why, you aren't black cats at all! You *are* rabbits!"

"As I said," countered Morel. "And we are wet and cold besides and would welcome a seat by your hearth."

"By all means," squeaked the mouse. "Bless me, I've forgotten my manners entirely! It's been simply ages since I entertained, you see. But do come in, and I'll have the kettle boiling straightaway."

The rabbits needed little encouragement and

soon found themselves seated in the tiny hovel, sipping dark green tea from tiny makeshift mugs.

"Seaweed tea." The mouse sighed. "It isn't overly tasty, but I'm afraid it's all I've got."

"I rather like it," said Leek. This wasn't entirely true, of course, as seaweed tea is something of an acquired taste. But Leek didn't want to be rude. That was Morel's department.

"What is your name, mouse?" demanded Morel. "And how came you to the belly of this dark beast?"

"My name is Hamlin." The little mouse sighed. "I am a wandering minstrel, or at least I was, and rather a good one, if I do say so myself. Why, there was a time when I played for very important rodents, of the very highest quality. But a wandering minstrel wanders, you see, by definition, and earns his daily crumb by luck, on a road that never ends. Yet perhaps you know, as wayfarers yourselves, that the road is not always kind."

"Of this"—Morel frowned—"we are aware."

"It was a dark and stormy night," continued Hamlin. "The hail came down as big as . . . well, as big as me—and bigger. I was all alone in an unfamiliar land and soaked to the tip of my tail. But in the distance,

I saw a snatch of light and made for it posthaste, in hope of warmth and cheer. As I approached, I soon beheld a caravan—rather a ramshackle affair, to be frank, but a caravan nonetheless—and crept inside. Its sole occupant was a conjurer of sorts—and not a well-mannered conjurer by any standard! Though wet and bedraggled, I pulled out my flute and embarked on a merry tune. But rather than clapping and cutting the cheese, the conjurer reached for his broom."

"Imbrolio." Leek shuddered. "It could only be he."

"I was forced to flee for my life," moaned Hamlin, "and leaped into a hat. And the next thing I knew, a legion of black cats was chasing me through a world without a sun. A harrowing affair, to say the absolute least, and me with only a flute for protection!"

"Flutes make very ineffective weapons," agreed Morel, "especially small ones."

"They chased me to the water's edge, where I was forced to swim, only to be swallowed by this loathsome fish. And I've been here ever since. It is a terrible fate, and yet the beast provides safe haven from the cats, for which I must be grateful."

Leek sighed and politely sipped his tea. The mouse had experienced the very worst sort of luck, for cats hate mice even worse than lucky rabbits. Hamlin couldn't possibly have found himself in a more inhospitable realm. But Leek liked the little mouse, and he was glad to have him as a friend.

"My name is Leek," said Leek. "And this is my guide, Morel. Together, we are on a mission. We seek a dark, mysterious tower within the fortress of the cats, where it's said there's a way back home. I'd very much like you to join us. One never knows when a minstrel might come in handy."

Morel raised an eyebrow. As far as she could tell, their mission had come to a definite and decidedly unpleasant end. Hamlin's shoulders slumped in obvious agreement.

"Thank you very much," said the mouse. "But I am afraid of cats, as well as their towers and fortresses. And even if I was a brave mouse warrior rather than a musician, the fact remains that we are held captive in the belly of a fish. There's no way out. I've looked."

"There's always a way with luck." Leek smiled.

"I *would* like to see the sun again," admitted Hamlin. "And the tale of our escape would make for a wonderful song. But my luck has met its end, here beneath the sea, and so has yours."

Hamlin suddenly felt such a terrible sense of desperation that he turned from the rabbits to cry. His sadness had been bearable, in a way, when he was alone, if only because he didn't have to talk about it. But then his guests had come, and manners dictated that he answer their questions willingly and honestly. Answering questions meant he was forced to recount, and in some ways relive, all the very worst moments of his life. The moments all gathered in two little glands behind his eyes, then oozed out in great wet drops, which trickled down his whiskers in such numbers that Hamlin soon felt rather dehydrated.

Just as the last tear wound its way slowly down Hamlin's longest whisker, Leek reached out and brushed his back with a paw, offering small comfort and something more besides.

"Terribly sorry," said the mouse, wiping his eyes. "I really ought to serve a bit of a bite, I suppose. I haven't much, but I have been experimenting with seaweed cheese. It isn't half bad, all things considered."

Morel wrinkled her nose. Seaweed cheese didn't sound all that appetizing. And, in truth, it isn't.

"That's very kind," she said in her most diplomatic tone, "but we have brought provisions, of which you are welcome to partake."

With that, she withdrew her pouch of neeps. But just as Morel loosened the cord that held the satchel tight, the great fish turned abruptly from its course, and the satchel fell to the floor, spilling the dried rutabaga hither and yon. Just like that, seaweed cheese was immediately back on the menu. Morel sighed heavily, then sighed all over again. More bad luck, she thought. Just when things couldn't possibly get any worse, they got worse.

Suddenly, the cavern shook, with a tremor that on a scale of one to ten would have registered a resounding twelve and a half. Leek, Morel, and Hamlin found themselves flying past one another and bouncing against the walls of the little shack.

"Out!" commanded Morel. "Before it collapses upon us!"

Hamlin snatched his trusty flute, the one thing in his life untarnished by ill luck, and the troop bounded out of his rough home just as it shuddered and collapsed in a heap.

"What," yelped Hamlin, "was that?"

Before Leek could even think to offer a guess, there came another tremor and another and many more. As he was tossed about the cavernous gut of the beast, Leek glimpsed two furry shapes whizzing past him at speed, which he took to be his friends. This is a most unexpected turn of events, he thought as he careened past a fleshy stalactite.

The tremors subsided just briefly, and Leek rose from the pit of that great stomach, turning to Hamlin and smiling in sudden revelation.

"I believe our fish is sneezing."

"Sneezing!" cried the mouse. "But what possible allergen could cause a giant fish to sneeze?"

Morel stared at Leek in sudden wonder. She had seen him touch the mouse, but she hadn't thought much of it at the time. Now she knew what Leek had done. And what's more, she knew just what foreign allergen had caused the fish to sneeze. As the last and greatest tremor rocked the cavern, sending the mouse and both rabbits up and out of the fish, into the indigo sky and past the ever-present moon, Morel called out:

"NEEPS!"

Precisely six seconds later, the threesome landed

in a furry little mound on the far shore of the Great Ink, where precious few rabbits—and certainly no mouse—had ever laid a paw. But Leek, you understand, was a very persistent sort of lucky rabbit. After all, he had a little boy to think about.

CHAPTER FOUR

Cecil Bean, in the meantime, had embarked on an adventure all his own, in search of the Great Imbrolio. He had stuffed his pockets with all the things he thought an adventure might require, including a pocketknife, a bit of twine, and one spare pair of tighty-whities, as well as four fresh slices of whole-wheat bread, and eight cross sections of thinly sliced salami. Cecil had elected to wear a dark blue anorak with a hood, which seemed like it might offer some degree of invisibility, were the boy given opportunity to sneak up on Imbrolio deep in the shadow of night. He had also decided to wear two pairs of socks, but that was just because it was chilly.

Cecil had been walking all day and had passed through two small villages, much like his own, where he duly noted signs of Imbrolio's passage. In the first, Cecil spied a tiny girl caked in mud, staring up through cracked glasses at the remains of her kite, which had been shredded irrevocably by an osprey. In the second, Cecil watched as a boy his own age sprinted by naked as a jaybird and covered in black molasses, pursued by a swarm of bees. The villain Imbrolio had left a trail of ill luck, all too easy to follow. So Cecil pressed on, farther than he had ever traveled before, emboldened by the knowledge that there were other victims who desperately needed his help, in addition to their rabbits.

As he walked, Cecil pondered at length the mysterious gentleman he'd met at his favorite café. Why was it, wondered Cecil, that the man's own rabbit had retired? What precisely was the secret that had freed him from the whims of his cat? And why on earth, wondered Cecil Bean, must the magician's code be so exceedingly stringent?

The orange sun sank lazily behind the hill beyond the meadow, where Cecil suddenly found himself exhausted, alone, and increasingly cold. So the boy sank into a warm bed of russet-red leaves, in the hollow of an ancient tree, and peeked out from the hood of his anorak as the stars took their places in the sky. Before sleep took him, one bright star shot across his field of vision, trailing a streak of bright white. And as Cecil closed his eyes, he made a wish.

"I wish," whispered the boy, "that I was a magician, too. For then I'd have mysterious secrets of my own. And I would only ever share them with my rabbit."

"The Jungle Prime Evil," said Morel. "Legends speak of the perils that await within."

"What sorts of perils, precisely?" asked Leek, who still smelled strongly of fish.

"The legends," whispered Morel, narrowing her eyes, "are unspecific."

"Well," said Leek with a smile, "I suppose the answers to such questions lie in courage. So we'd best be off, then, hadn't we?"

"Wait," squeaked Hamlin. "I am compelled to

thank you both. And though the aid of one small mouse may hardly seem like much, I hereby pledge it to you, with allegiance evermore, until my debt is paid."

"That's awfully good of you to say," said Leek, rather moved by Hamlin's speech. "We accept your offer with great honor and humility."

Leek and Hamlin shook paws with a great deal of bowing and formality thrown in for good measure, and as they did, Morel considered their plight. Though Hamlin was a very small mouse to be sure, he was yet another mouth to feed. What's more, Hamlin, by his own admission, was merely a musician. A warrior would be one thing, armed with a halberd or mace, but Morel doubted a flautist would be much use at all.

"If the Dimmer-Dammers catch us," she muttered under her breath, "he can play our swan song."

The fellowship of three strode forward into the jungle, led by a rabbit who doubted their luck would hold. But still she had her spear and sword. And a stout blade, considered Morel, just might be luck enough.

Leek's approach was rather less considered. His only thoughts were of Cecil.

The jungle soon enveloped them, dense and cruel and dark. The thorns of trees were big as spikes, the vines thick as the largest of snakes—and some equally poisonous. High above them, moonbeams pierced the pitiless canopy, spotting the forest floor in polka dots of doom. Morel was pleased to note that there seemed a path of sorts, but even as she stared ahead, it seemed to almost slither—and wind in ways that made the warrior wary.

The path was the least of her worries. Strange sounds soon reached her ears: squawks and snorts and squeaks. Some such sounds seemed surprisingly close, often just inches away. But every time Morel twirled and turned, she saw only her companions, following close behind.

Once, and only once, Morel might have sworn she heard the snuffling of a pig—and glimpsed the telltale gleam of beady, porcine eyes. But she dismissed the notion at once. This was the dominion of cats and cats alone.

The path squirmed upward, and summoning their strength, Hamlin and Leek strove hard to stay close to their guide. As they crested the rise, Morel suddenly crouched and motioned her friends to be silent. For there below them, rising from the undergrowth, stood a solitary outpost. And even from a distance, its stench was ripe with warning.

"What is it?" whispered Leek.

"A watchtower," said Morel, wrinkling her nose with foreboding. "And it stinks of cat. The path has betrayed us."

"Then we must stray from the path," said Leek, "and trust ourselves to luck."

"Of all the rabbits condemned to life in Hat, I have always proved most willing to seek another way," said Morel. "But I am a stranger to the Jungle Prime Evil, and to stray from this trail might well prove our ruin."

Leek smiled. "Nonsense. You must simply follow your spear, and we will follow you, our guide in whom we trust."

Hamlin nodded in agreement, and so the vote was cast. They dared not creep too close to the tower of the cats; that much was all too clear. But which way, then, to go? Morel just wasn't sure. So she spoke unto her spear.

"Great spear, old friend," she whispered to its shaft, "I trust the path to you. I beg you point the way, and do not fail."

Morel thus closed her eyes and gripped her weapon tight—and of its own accord, the spearpoint pointed right.

"We will go right," spoke Morel in resolution.

"Of course we will," said Leek. "Things always go right, with luck."

Leek was unaware that high above them a scouting Dimmer-Dammer, soaring noiseless on the wind, had spied the faint glint of steel, as well as the fellowship it briefly alit, and returned to its roost to report. For luck, as you well know, comes in two distinct varieties. And within the world of Hat, they seldom rise in equal measure.

As the trio pressed on, deeper into the jungle, even Leek's eternal optimism soon sputtered and went out. With every step, his paws recoiled at the bites of rock and thorn, and poor Hamlin, small as he was, soon proved the worse for wear. The little mouse did not complain, but his stomach rebelled against him, growling for attention.

"You would think," whimpered Hamlin, "that

even an evil jungle might bear a bit of fruit. We haven't had a thing since teatime. Teatime yesterday, come to think of it!"

"Let your hunger fuel your courage," said Morel. "We will be lean and mean."

But Morel had to admit that she was hungry, too. Only the memory of her human girl drove her forward. It had been years since they had parted, and as Morel pressed on through vines before her, she suddenly recalled her human's love of orchards. The girl had always been partial to a very specific fruit, and when she walked among the trees, Morel had followed close behind, making sure that only the very finest specimens fell at her charge's feet. The recollection was a warm one, from an age almost forgotten, so strong that Morel could almost smell it.

"Apple," she said to herself, and sighed.

"I'm not quite sure what it is," said Leek, "but it *does* rather smell like an apple!"

Morel snapped from her reverie and stared ahead. Not fifty feet before her was a clearing, and sitting in a narrow shaft of moonlight was just what she had smelled: a sort of apple. Yet the apple was nearly black in color, and something about its odor just didn't smell quite right.

"Well, whatever it is, I think it smells delicious!" cried Hamlin, his belly gurgling in agreement. With that, the mouse rushed forward, with Leek in eager tow. An apple, of all things! Luck was with them after all, even in the Jungle Prime Evil.

As the pair rushed toward their prize, Morel's whiskers twitched with apprehension. And suddenly, she dashed for her friends, for she had recognized the smell that wasn't right, masked as it was by the apple.

Before she could even cry out, a great net sprang from a patch of black leaves. Morel's sword and spear fell to the earth, as did the traitorous apple, and the companions could only stare down, suspended as they were, as dark forms gathered beneath them.

The smell Morel had smelled was a trap.

Cruelly gagged and tightly bound, the companions soon found themselves tied by all fours to a stick, which Morel recognized with a grimace as her spear. From her spear they dangled while small figures, masked in shadow, carried them through the bush.

Morel twisted and writhed, but the vines that held her were far too strong to break. And the bitter gag in her mouth prevented her from voicing all manner of nasty remarks. At last she relented and ceased to struggle. She would wait, conserving her strength, and hope for some later chance to fight back.

It didn't take long for the prisoners to lose all sense of direction—and then, one by one, to nod in sleep. Hamlin was plagued by nightmarish dreams and shuddered more than once in abject fear.

Leek, on the other hand, enjoyed rather pleasant dreams of his boy. But he awakened with a start when dropped roughly to the ground, then thoroughly prodded and poked. Bound though he was, Leek sat upright to gaze at the figure doing the poking.

It was a pig.

The pig was painted with tribal markings and sculptured ornaments dangled from its snout and ears. The pig wore little in the way of clothing, and naught but a slight breechcloth concealed its jiggly bits. But what was most remarkable about the pig was its size. It was scarcely taller than Hamlin—though substantially more menacing.

Leek gasped. "Who, or what, are you?"

"I am Kadogo," snorted the pig, "king of the Miniature Potbellies."

"Well, my name is Leek," replied the rabbit, "and I don't much like to be poked."

"You are not very fat," said Kadogo. "But this will please my physician. She's very concerned about my cholesterol."

"I demand to be released this very instant," cried Leek. "My companions and I have no argument with you or your tribe."

"The warrior does," said Kadogo, grinning and gesturing at Morel. "In fact, we had to replace her gag. She is very rude."

"Yes, sometimes," admitted Leek. "But she's quite essential to my journey. She's my guide, you know."

"Not anymore," snorted Kadogo. "Henceforth, she shall be known as supper!"

"Supper!" exclaimed Leek. "But surely you don't mean . . ."

"Silence!" bellowed Kadogo. "You stink of sea monster! And now you shall suffer the fate of all who trespass in my realm. It's bath time!"

At this, the dozens of surrounding potbellies burst into laughter and cheers. Several rushed forth, bearing wood and tinder, which soon produced a blaze. Atop the fire was placed a massive cauldron, filled to the brim with broth, which quickly simmered and steamed. And to Leek's horror, his captors hoisted the threesome aloft, then plopped them in, one by one, to cook. Leek's paws were still bound, and Morel's rough gag was still tied tightly in place. Leek's last hopes soon commenced to drift away, with the smell of boiling rabbit.

But as Kadogo danced past the great vat, Leek just managed to reach out and brush his hide with a paw.

Suddenly, a small voice rang out, clear and high, above the drums and chants of the prancing potbellies.

"Wait!" cried Hamlin the mouse. "I have a last request!"

Kadogo turned, and with a wave of his hoof, the potbellied camp went silent.

"Name any boon but mercy," said Kadogo, "and I will grant it."

"Great king," spoke Hamlin in a slow and steady voice, "this is all a terrible mistake. To these two rabbits, I owe a debt, which I fear now may never be paid. Thus I humbly ask, mighty Kadogo, that I may honor them, in this their final hour, with the last of my meager breath."

Morel, though gagged and bound, rolled her eyes at Hamlin's request, and Kadogo laughed with a hearty oink.

"Even denied a voice, the she-rabbit is rude! But so let it be. We will hear you, little mouse, before we eat our stew."

With that, Kadogo drew a long stone knife from his waist and cut through Hamlin's bonds. The mouse paused, then raised himself to the edge of the pot, to play with pride one final time. From his fur, he pulled his flute, which sparkled with moonlight and flame. Kadogo narrowed his eyes, awaiting what would come, and as fiery embers leaped toward the heavens, Hamlin's last song began.

The melody was but a simple one, which Hamlin had never played before. Some songs lie dormant in a minstrel's heart, you see, often for many years. And some, quite sadly, never emerge at all—and remain unplayed forever. But others, and often the very

finest sorts, simply wait until the time is right. This was the sort of tune that sprang from Hamlin's flute, and the tribe of Kadogo gasped at its pure beauty. To the miniature potbellies, and to Leek and even Morel, it was a song that reached into the hidden valleys of their souls and banished all sadness, however briefly. Kadogo felt that he was floating, and the thick ridge of coarse hair that ran the length of his back tingled and stood on end. He hoped the song would never end.

The mouse played on, his eyes shut tight, as the song spilled forth from his heart. This was his gift to Leek and Morel, and he had nothing greater to give.

As the melody poured out deep into the night, even the moonlight felt warm. For the beams absorbed the song, and with it, Hamlin's noble spirit. And in the few small spots along the forest floor where the moonlight touched the earth, the black rock trembled, as if touched from far beneath.

From these spots emerged small fungi—deep, dark blue in color—which sprang forth in search of the song.

As the final notes of Hamlin's song floated into the

air and away, Kadogo opened his eyes knowing that somehow an emptiness inside him had been filled. But as the great chief gazed about him, he blinked and blinked again in disbelief.

"The truffles," he gasped. "The truffles have returned."

CHAPTER FIVE

Millikin hissed and spat, the hapless villain beside himself with rage. As he stormed through the black citadel of the cats, his brethren leaped from his path. Millikin was so angry, you see, even his friends were afraid.

When the scout had returned, Millikin was just preparing to enter the tower and return to the business of Cecil Bean. Then the news had come that, although recently devoured by a carnivorous aquatic monster of prehistoric proportion, Leek and the she-rabbit had just been spotted in the jungle. What's more, they were apparently traveling with a mouse, adding considerable insult to Millikin's already injured pride.

At this rate, everyone in Hat would be laughing at Millikin's expense—and if somehow Leek should actually breach the fortress, an unthinkable circumstance altogether, well, then Millikin figured he might as well just give up entirely and go live in a hole, eat slugs, grow an enormous beard, and compose depressing poetry no one would ever read.

But Leek would never breach the fortress, Millikin assured himself. The jungle paths all led to heavily fortified outposts, and of course there were always the potbellies. Their pathetic little weapons were no match for even the smallest of Dimmer-Dammers, to be sure, and their numbers had dwindled substantially since the disappearance of the truffles. But still, thought Millikin, the pigs were ruthless fighters and could surely be counted on to hunt and dispatch two small rabbits and a mouse.

But Millikin wasn't leaving the matter of Leek to chance. Thus, he strode to the launch port, his sinister black tail commanding his allies to follow. There,

Millikin leaped astride a great iron raptor, terror of the skies and harbinger of ruin.

"Mount the Dimmer-Dammers, soldiers of darkness," he cried, "and take to the wind! The rabbit Leek yet lives, and on his head, I will rain my vengeance!

"And maybe," he whispered to himself, "maybe then I will be happy."

"Truffles are quite timid, you see," explained Kadogo. "It doesn't take much to frighten a truffle."

Leek nodded and rubbed his wrists, which still bore the marks of sticky bonds. Morel sat close nearby, sharpening her spear with a stone, and Hamlin reclined in honor on a comfy bed of leaves to the right of the potbellied king. The remainder of Kadogo's tribe milled about among the truffles, breathing in the earthy scent for which they long had yearned.

"My people have tracked the truffle herd for countless generations, on its long migrations throughout the Jungle Prime Evil. And in our travels, we have always been content, for it is the way of the pig to wander. Since time began, we have hunted the truffles as nomads, eating those of age and dressing ourselves in their hides."

"You eat them?" Leek gasped. "Well, then it isn't any wonder that they're frightened! I'd be timid, too, were I a truffle!"

"Ah," said Kadogo, "but the truffles want to be eaten. It is a matter of multiplication."

"I see," said Leek, though he didn't see, exactly, quite what the great king meant.

"We miniature potbellies, you understand, are born as boars or sows, just like rabbits."

"I am no sow," snapped Morel.

"But truffles," continued Kadogo, "are simply truffles. They are not male or female. They do not date or fall in love, and as such, they are quite incapable of multiplication. At least, that is to say, they cannot multiply without our help. Potbellies and truffles enjoy a symbiotic relationship." (Which is a five-dollar way of saying that the pigs and truffles need each other—and that both get something good out of the bargain.)

"When a truffle is ready, a pig gladly eats that truffle. And when it passes through us (manners prevent me from offering greater detail), then the truffle's spores are both fertilized and spread. A thousand truffle infants thusly result, to take their places within the herd."

As if on cue, a truffle trundled up to the side of the great king and leaped happily into his mouth.

"And so," said Kadogo with a smile, "the circle of life goes on."

But the great king's face grew dark. "Yet times have changed, with the advent of feline technologies. Always have we shared this land with the cats, each tribe simply going about its business, in the ways that Mother Moon deems fit. But the cats have grown too great, driven by their lust for ill luck, which has gone too long unchecked. Now their Dimmer-Dammers rend the stillness of the night. Their great roars frighten the truffles—and send them deep into the earth, beyond the reach of even our most skillful snouts. For long years have I, Kadogo, sought some means to bring them forth again, and always have I failed. But on this hallowed eve, fair Hamlin, you have brought us sweet reunion. Of your gift shall we sing until the potbellies are no more."

"We didn't really want to eat you," added the king, with just a touch of sheepishness. "Rabbit's a bit gamey for my taste anyway."

"Well," said Leek, smiling. "No harm done, and no offense taken. I actually think bacon smells lovely, though of course I'm strictly vegan."

"May your gardens always bear fruit," said Kadogo. "And now, friend Leek, how may the tribe of Kadogo aid you in your quest?"

"We seek the fortress of the cats," said Morel in a low tone that made Kadogo cringe.

"Then you seek your end, and I would not see you perish," replied the king. "Rather, I invite you to join our clan. Roam the jungle with us. Always are warriors welcome in the tribe of King Kadogo."

"Thank you ever so much," said Leek. "But I really must return to my boy in the world that I call home. As far as I'm concerned, it's basically the big creepy tower or bust."

"Yet to reach the tower," whispered Kadogo, "you must pass through the Grottos of Ill Repute, where there is only darkness."

"Well, it was pretty dark inside our sea monster," said Leek. "How bad can it really be?"

"Ah, but friend Leek," said Kadogo. "It is not the darkness you must fear, but he who waits within. For it is said that deep down in the caves there lurks an ancient evil. Often have we heard his howls, of hunger and of rage."

Just then, far away, there came a cry of despair, a gruesome wail that made the rabbits' blood run cold. Leek couldn't help but shudder, a foreboding chill seeping through his every vein, but Morel simply stood and raised her spear.

"Is there no other way?" she demanded of the chieftain.

"There is none, she-rabbit. Your path leads only down, where even truffles fear to tread."

"Then we go down," said Morel, "to face what lies before us. I do not fear the darkness or that which waits within, for I am Morel. And I have spoken."

"So let it be," decreed Kadogo, who didn't savor the thought of an argument with Morel. "We shall lead you to the entrance of that evil lair and mourn your passing in song."

"There's been quite enough song for one night," replied Morel, rolling her eyes. And with that, she strode forth, past the warmth of the fire, toward the cry that still echoed in her ears.

Cecil had risen early, a bit stiff but otherwise intact. The boy quickly fortified himself with a sandwich, which he cut in two neat pieces with his pocketknife. Part of him might have enjoyed a mug of hot tea, with a liberal dollop of honey, but whatever part of him that was, Cecil decided to ignore. Sometimes, Cecil reasoned, an adventurer must forego such comforts in pursuit of greater goals. And Cecil's goal, which loomed large before him, was to track the villain Imbrolio and the hat that wasn't his.

So Cecil Bean walked straight toward the horizon, which is where adventure always lies, following the trail of bad luck through every town he entered. Cecil could only note the villagers' assorted troubles, as some unfolded right before his eyes. And though he couldn't be entirely certain, he felt sure he was getting close. For unlike the Not-So-Great Imbrolio, Cecil never stopped to trap rabbits or perform lackluster tricks. He paused only to sleep, and even then, it was little more than a power nap. Otherwise, Cecil simply walked and walked, and once his sandwich had properly digested, he even jogged a bit.

But again, as had happened the day before, Cecil walked all day with nary a glimpse of his quarry's dilapidated caravan. Dusk settled like a thick woolen blanket over the sprawling forest ahead, and Cecil took careful note of dark clouds that gathered in warning of storm. As the first great drops fell heavily upon him, Cecil peered into the soupy gloom, hoping for yet another hollow tree in which to weather the night. Of course, thought Cecil, that would take some luck, of which he seemed in short supply.

Then, through the murk, he spied the bright blue flame of a cookstove.

Cecil crept forward with the stealth of an assassin and soon beheld the garish silhouette of a caravan. The boy caught his breath at the sight, lest his prey should detect him. But all stayed still, and when Cecil dared to breathe again, his nose caught a toothsome scent.

Sausages, thought Cecil. The cheeky brigand is grilling sausages—fresh pork, I'd say, by the smell of them.

"I can smell it, too." Leek shuddered.

Led by Kadogo and his warriors, the companions had traveled countless leagues through the dark heart of the jungle, following no proper path so far as

Morel could discern. But to Kadogo, the path was all too obvious. For the sovereign's sensitive snout now followed a very specific stench, which grew stronger as they walked. Soon even Hamlin's small nose recoiled in frank rebellion.

"I smell the reek of great unhappiness," whispered the mouse. "And I fear this putrid funk as I have feared no other. Why, it's worse than cat pee!"

"You are right to fear, my friend," said Kadogo, "for you smell your own undoing."

Then, as if repelled by the rotten odor in the air, the trees themselves gave way to barren desert, at the center of which was a hole. From its depths rose dark green vapors, which assaulted the travelers with the grim scent of despondence—which is to say it smelled very bad indeed.

"There lies the path," said Kadogo. "And I beg you yet again, my friends, to stay with us and live in honor much deserved."

"Thank you, O king, for all that you have done," said Leek. "But now our ways must part. Should we fare well, my companions and myself, we have only you to thank."

"And should we not," said Morel, "it will be our

courage, and not Kadogo, that has failed us."

Kadogo smiled. "You speak fair words, and in thanks, I now bestow such gift as only a king may offer."

Kadogo then held forth an earthen jug marked with the rune-sign of his people. Tiny holes were pierced in its lid, for that which was within was alive.

"Inside this sacred vessel, I have placed my greatest treasure, held within since I was but a piglet. For every king, before he may ascend our throne, must prove himself by surviving alone in the infinite jungle for twelve moons, with only his bow and his wits to guard him in time of need."

"This custom seems just," said Morel, "for only the worthy may lead."

"My trial was a cruel one," continued Kadogo, "and I wandered to the darkest corners of this land. But it was there, where even my bright spirit dwindled and nearly went out, that I beheld two spheres of glowing light dancing before me—held aloft by some forgotten brand of sorcery. These lights gave me comfort and rekindled the flame within my breast. So I took them from the air and returned in triumph to my people. To this day, they burn with a hope that may never be extinguished. My father, in his final breath, spoke of a vision and said my hope had come to me from a land beyond my own. This land, I think, must also be yours as well, lucky Leek and brave Morel. Thus I give the gift of light to you who dare to walk so deep. May it serve you well."

"Your light shall shine upon my spear," said Morel, "and give it greater glory."

"Yes, thank you very much," added Leek. "It's a lovely present."

Just then, a shadow passed across the moon of Hat. Kadogo's hairy spine bristled in sudden alarm, and his keen black eyes narrowed as he looked to the sky.

"The Dimmer-Dammers are upon us!" he snarled. "Into the abyss, before they descend, or your quest ends here and now!"

"I will not shrink from battle!" yelled Morel. "Let them come and feel my wrath!"

"Nay, shield-maiden of the rabbits," said Kadogo, a twinkle in his eye. "Trust now in the might of our potbellied bows. Continue on your quest, and return to the world where you belong."

The Dimmer-Dammers dropped from the sky in droves, their engines shrieking with hate. The beating of their loathsome wings lashed the troupe with the force of a thousand storms while their churning gears croaked warning of death from above.

On the foremost of these beasts rode Millikin, with wrath in his eyes and malice in his heart. Baring his fangs, he called out to those who followed behind.

"One metric ton of catnip for he who brings me Leek! Disgrace, dishonor, and dismemberment for all who allow his escape! Attack! Attack without mercy or restraint! And, needless to say, no quarter for the mouse!"

"What good are bows against this fearsome flock?" demanded Hamlin. "Your arrows are no match for iron hides!"

"Their armor may be thick, friend Hamlin," said Kadogo, fitting a dart to his bowstring, "but even machines must breathe. So we will aim for their snouts."

Kadogo loosed his arrow, which sprang noiselessly, swift and true, streaking across the sky toward the Dimmer-Dammer at Millikin's left. Its pilot could only curse as the dart found its mark, plugging the nostril of his mount. There it lodged, and the Dimmer-Dammer shuddered and burst with a piercing whistle of steam, its rider plunging into the jungle with a faint meow of fear. Hamlin had never dreamed of such a thing. And as the potbellied warriors sent forth a hail of darts, the mouse squeaked in sudden passion.

"Lend me a bow, Kadogo. This day, I will join you in battle, small as I may be."

"We potbellies have a saying before we go to war," said the chieftain, grinning. "Stature has nothing to do with it."

"Rabbits," cried Hamlin, "go now, in search of your humans, and think of me when you bring them fair luck!"

"We will," said Leek, roughly pushing Morel down into the hole. "May your deeds prove worthy of song!"

"There's been quite enough song for one night," said Hamlin as he sighted his bow to the sky. With that, the mouse fired upward at the largest of the Dimmer-Dammers, its cold, blank stare focused solely on its prey. The dart whistled softly into its mark, and when the Dimmer-Dammer fell to earth, its great bulk filled the hole where just a moment before, Hamlin's faithful friends had been.

Rising from the twisted wreck came Millikin, his cold, green eyes aflame with malice and rage. But even as he stared about him, at the mayhem he had wrought, he spied the glint of tribal arrows shining cold and merciless in the moonlight. As one, the arrows pointed toward him, held in check by stalwart hooves. And in a voice that quaked with shame, the savage cat cried out, "Dimmer-Dammers, retreat! The rabbit Leek has gone to certain death within the bowels of the earth! And now I, Millikin, purveyor of fates unfair and most unwelcome, shall return to Cecil Bean!"

"Begone, then, foul ravisher," spoke the great Kadogo. "Return to that dank underbelly from whence you lately came, and leave my pigs in peace."

Millikin eyed the chieftain, whose tusks seemed awfully sharp. Perhaps, he thought, he had rather underestimated the little pigs, who didn't seem so little anymore. But Millikin was not alone, as true cowards rarely are. And even as an iron bird swooped down to carry Millikin away, he spat a final parting.

"Swine! The ground you tread is my dominion, and you walk it at my whim. Pay tribute to your betters, or I shall lay waste the jungle—and all who dwell within! And as for you, little mouse, pathetic rodent that you are, our dispute is far from over."

"I should think not," said Hamlin as Millikin's curses faded into the distance. "I say, Kadogo! I rather like this battle business! And I simply love the smell of singed tomcat in the morning."

"It is not morning," said Kadogo grimly. "In my world, there is only night. And yet, friend Hamlin, most worthy of mice, I fear our friends may well be had for breakfast."

CHAPTER SIX

The Great Imbrolio yawned, picked his nose, and hung his undies to dry.

His sleep had been a fitful one, plagued by one highly disturbing dream, and though the man considered a catnap prior to breaking camp, he quickly decided against it. He didn't want to risk the dream again.

In the dream, an army of warriors laid siege to his caravan, surrounding it during the night. His tiny bedchamber had been pierced by a thousand spears, and Imbrolio had no choice but to stumble outside, clad only in his single pair of underwear, which he realized in dismay he had wet. There, beneath a sky that burned with flame, the warriors had gestured to his hat, which sat upside down, awaiting him. Somehow, the hat had grown to the size of a hot tub. On its brim, the warriors placed a plank, which Imbrolio was forced to walk as they jabbed at him and jeered. Imbrolio stumbled forward as the plank wobbled and bowed with his weight, and he looked down. Then he fell into the void and was gone.

No, decided Imbrolio, a catnap was most certainly out of the question.

So the man set about packing his small possessions and loading them into and onto his caravan. As he heaved an old black trunk high to the caravan's roof, it briefly crossed his mind that the trunk seemed unusually heavy. But then he remembered another detail of his dream.

The warriors had all had long ears.

Very strange, thought Imbrolio as he wiped the sweat from his brow. Very strange indeed—and far stranger than an unusually heavy trunk. No doubt he was simply tired after such a distressful night.

But Imbrolio knew what would make him feel better. Today, he would catch another rabbit, which he would subsequently thrust in his hat. How the crowd would cheer—for everyone loves magic. Imbrolio had always loved magic himself, which was why he had become such a very fine magician. Yes, of course that would make him feel better. It always did.

Imbrolio kicked his caravan, which sputtered and puttered to life, and squeezed himself into the cab. Yes, everything would be quite all right. All he needed to set his day in motion was a turnip, which he intended to steal at the very earliest opportunity.

So the caravan rolled slowly into the distance, slightly heavier than it had been the day before.

"Kadogo wasn't kidding," whispered Leek. "It's so black it's as if we're wearing sunglasses and trapped in a box at midnight. I suggest we use the chieftain's magic pot of light."

"We cannot risk this magic," said Morel, "lest it draw some evil to us."

"Oh," whispered Leek. "I hadn't thought of that."

"Which is why I do the thinking for us both," replied Morel. "No, we must make our way along the tunnel's wall, by touch, and stay wary of danger ahead."

"Quite right," said Leek. "Proceed."

But Morel had already proceeded, as was her way, and Leek hopped very quickly to catch up with her.

The stench belowground was overwhelming, and Morel secretly feared she might swoon. But she steeled herself against its onslaught and pressed on. She had faced many foes during her tenure in Hat, and it simply wouldn't do to be defeated by an odor. No one ever sings songs about warriors defeated by an odor, Morel considered, and when her time came at last to fall, she wanted to fall in battle, with honor. Her tribe could sing of that. That is, if they ever heard about it, which was another consideration altogether.

As they walked through the tunnel, hugging close to the relative safety of the wall, the stones they touched grew warmer with each step. Perhaps, thought Morel, as they crept deeper into Hat, they were nearing a geothermal pool or a lake of molten lava. There were many explanations for the warmth, and none of them were necessarily scary.

Then she heard a sound that was necessarily scary: the sound of breathing. With it came gusts of thick hot air, which explained the warmth of the walls.

"Where's that coming from?" squeaked Leek from behind her. "It smells awful."

"Keep quiet, and do as I say," came the rather rude response.

"Now wait just a minute," said Leek. "I almost always do as you say, and I feel compelled to note that just once, a 'please' would be greatly appreciated."

"Quiet, you fool!" said Morel.

"Well, now that isn't very nice at all," continued Leek, raising his voice. "I may not be a mighty warrior princess, but where I come from, we're taught to be polite. And I shan't go another step, or keep quiet, without a 'please.' I simply shan't."

But even if she'd wanted to say "please," which she didn't, Morel did not respond. For before she could even pause to be annoyed, there came a roar, which washed over the rabbits like a sonic wave of rage.

Morel took two steps back, and in the silence after, she dared to peer into the darkness ahead, where she caught sight of some shifting shadow.

"Run," she snapped to Leek. "Please."

Leek could not run, for his legs refused to move. In fact, Leek's fear was suddenly so great, he had forgotten he had legs at all, or what it even meant to run. It seemed to him that running was a concept he should know, but at present, all Leek could manage to do was tremble, from the tips of his whiskers to the end of his cotton-ball tail.

Morel did not tremble, for she knew her time had come. This was the moment for which her spear had waited, and this was the moment of which her clan would sing. But to merit such honor, she would have to summon a courage the likes of which she had never summoned before. As the shadow darkened before her, mammoth in size and nightmarish in shape, Morel thusly braced herself to fight for her life and for Leek's. Raising her weapon before her, she spoke as one must speak when certain doom awaits.

"Shadow of darkness," she yelled in a voice laden with grim resolve, "before you stands Morel, mightiest of rabbits within these savage lands, bearing both sword and spear!"

The black shape crept ever nearer, looming large beyond all reason, and much to his surprise, Leek's trembling suddenly stopped. Perhaps it was Morel.

Her courage could be infectious. But no, Leek realized, that wasn't it at all.

"From the depths may you emerge," Morel continued, "to prey upon the weak, but take warning and heed you well the words that I now speak. Oft have I roamed, to fight against all fear. And though I may fall this very day, you will find no weakness here."

The shadow cried out, turned tail, and ran.

Morel could not have been more surprised. It surprised her even more that precisely six seconds later, she found herself sprinting after it, bellowing a battle cry that shook the very walls around her. More surprising still was the fact that Leek was in front of her, running as only a rabbit can run.

The tunnel rose and dipped, and Leek slid down slippery slopes, with Morel close at his heels. Unlike his companion, Leek yelled no mighty battle cry. He had no wish for battle. No, Leek had something altogether different in mind for the shadow before him, and as he gained upon its bulk, he reached out, even as he ran, and brushed its back with his paw.

With a resounding crash and a yelp of pain, the shadow misjudged the tunnel's path and collided soundly with its wall. Leek, in turn, collided with the shadow, and Morel collided with Leek—nearly skewering him with her spear.

Such was the force of that fateful collision that the sacred urn of King Kadogo was crushed to smithereens.

In the silence that followed, two tiny orbs of light came forth, followed by dozens more. And as the tunnel grew ever brighter, the tiny spheres rose, as one, to the monster's gruesome head, for the shadow was shadow no more. Great horns sprouted gigantic from a sea of tousled mane, and warts the size of Leek himself adorned the monster's chin. As the monster's eyes grew wide in curious wonder, the lights rose around him, and formed a sort of crown.

Leek gasped. "They're fireflies!"

"I think you're right," whispered Morel. "But I thought Kadogo said that there were only two."

"Why," said Leek in realization, "they must have multiplied!"

"Beautiful," said the monster. "So small and yet so bright. What luck that here, among the caves, these lights should come to me."

(Though unable to voice their joy, lacking in vocal cords of course, the fireflies were pleased as well. The fireflies had been courting, you see, long ago, in the world that has a sun. And over time, the two had fallen in love and been married. But the he-fly lived on only a modest income, and a honeymoon abroad was quite beyond his means. So the he-fly and the she-fly had decided to leave their accommodations to chance and simply go on a walkabout prior to set-tling down. So it was that they had come to rest in a hat, with rather unexpected results. And soon enough, they found themselves placed in an earthen jug, which certainly had its charms but lacked in ade-quate closet space. When the she-fly revealed that she was with child, her husband was overjoyed, to be sure. But his true love's talk of a cozy nest, where her nesting instinct might reach suitable fruition, worried him to the point of desperation. When his children finally came, one after another after several dozen more, quarters became very tight indeed.

Yet now, before them, was a great mane of tou-sled hair, warm and wholly inviting, where the pair could raise their young and live happily ever after. The she-fly even thought they might build a little cottage, with a white picket fence, and the he-fly announced that he would go to the local shelter and adopt a flea. His wife agreed, on condition that her husband look after its droppings.)

The monster sighed in quiet reverie, enchanted by the light, then abruptly remembered his manners. And turning to the tiny brown rabbits standing betwixt his toes, he spoke in humble tones.

"Hello," he said. "I am a cave monster, and my name is Gordon."

"Hello," said Leek, smiling. "My name is Leek, and this is my guide, Morel."

"They're wonderful, aren't they?" whispered Gordon. "Little dancing lights."

"Marvelous," agreed Leek. "My boy, Cecil Bean, loves fireflies, too."

"Just a moment," interrupted Morel. "What kind of cave monster are you, anyway? Every cave monster I've ever heard of would have eaten us by now! Why, we heard your roars and growls many leagues from here, deep in the Jungle Prime Evil!"

"Oh, those weren't roars or growls," said Gordon rather shyly. "Those were moans of fear."

"Fear!" gasped Morel. "But you're a cave monster, ten times the size of any Dimmer-Dammer in existence, with horns and great big muscles! What in all of Hat has such a mighty beast to fear?"

"Well, you see," said Gordon in his most timid voice, "I am afraid of the dark."

Cecil Bean was not afraid of the dark, but he had to admit that it did make sandwich construction difficult. The trunk in which he'd stowed away was relatively comfortable, all things considered, but he had reached the last of his provisions and certainly didn't want to waste them. There's little worse than a poorly constructed sandwich, and Cecil was a stickler when it came to sandwiches. So he concentrated very hard as he constructed his.

As Cecil munched away, however, he began to think of the many things he did fear. He feared needles a bit, especially when stuck in his arm. And he rather feared beards, for some odd reason. But most of all, Cecil feared failure. For should he fail, then he and his lucky rabbit would never see each other again. To prevent such a dismal prospect from occurring, Cecil realized, he would need two things.

First, he would have to figure out the great secret of the mysterious gentleman, over whom luck seemed to hold no sway. The last thing Cecil needed, you see, was a stroke of bad luck just as he was preparing to save his rabbit. That could prove disastrous.

The other thing he'd need, of course, was the magic word required to operate the hat—and execute rabbit extraction. But with considered regard to this part, Cecil decided he would simply have to trust to trial and error. And maybe, just maybe, he'd get lucky.

Millikin had had every intention of returning to Cecil's village and to Cecil, for whom he had planned a variety of deliciously nasty tricks. But as he strode for the great black tower, which contained his means of transport to the boy, a nagging doubt tugged at the base of his brain.

Everyone knew that the Grottos of Ill Repute were haunted by a monster of gargantuan size with an appetite to match. Millikin himself had often heard its cries of rage, which made Millikin's tail puff out to the size of a feather boa. But since Millikin hadn't actually seen the rabbits mashed and gnashed between the monster's five-foot fangs, he couldn't be certain that Leek was truly gone forever. He'd thought he'd vanquished his foe when Leek was engulfed by the fish. Yet Leek had soon reappeared in the jungle, with his girlfriend and mouse in tow. Then Millikin had assured himself that surely the filthy pigs, in their hunger, would catch the meddlesome trio—and promptly boil them alive. Yet the potbellies had not only failed to boil them, they'd escorted them straight to the caves.

No, thought Millikin, Cecil Bean would have to wait. He simply couldn't return to work until he was sure, very sure, that Leek had met his end. So Millikin turned on his heels and walked briskly toward the product development lab, where he'd heard that a menacing new brand of Dimmer-Dammer was underway. Some cats enjoyed referring to the new prototype as a "Digger-Dammer," but Millikin frowned on the term. The cats, in Millikin's considered opinion, had spent a great deal of time and effort building their brand equity, and he didn't like to muddy the market with new and confusing names, however catchy.

Imagine, thought Millikin, descending on some hapless victim, only to hear him scream the wrong thing.

CHAPTER SEVEN

"It is a terrible thing to be afraid of the dark," confessed the monstrous Gordon, "particularly when one resides in a cave."

Gordon sat on his haunches so as to converse more easily with his guests. As he spoke, the light of the fireflies shone brightly against the black rock all around them, which sparkled as if in thanks. Leek felt awfully glad to have made a new friend, especially such a big one. And Morel, for her part, felt awfully glad she hadn't had to fight the mammoth beast. She was certain that, if properly provoked, Gordon would make a formidable foe. Yet there was something she couldn't quite grasp about his dilemma.

"But why not simply leave the caves," she asked, "and roam the surface, where at least there is the moon to light your way?"

"I am a cave monster," said Gordon, shrugging, "and so by definition, I must live in my cave. I've always assumed that roaming the surface wasn't allowed."

"Well, I highly recommend it, should you ever reconsider," said Leek. "We met some lovely potbellies in the jungle."

"You don't eat pork, do you?" inquired Morel, fearing for Kadogo and his tribe.

"I don't think so," said Gordon, who had always considered himself a vegetarian. "But now that I have the little dancing lights, the caves don't seem so bad."

"Gordon," spoke Leek, choosing his words with care, "we couldn't help but notice an unsettling aroma when we entered your subterranean realm. It's remarkably pungent."

"Oh, I suppose that's probably me." Gordon sighed, and as he sighed, a fresh wave of green vapor washed over the rabbits. "In addition to my nyctophobia"—which is a five-dollar word for fear of the dark—"I also suffer from simple chronic halitosis"—which is the five-dollar way dental technicians refer to bad breath.

Leek thought instantly of the large patch of mint that grew wild in the field behind Cecil's home and made a mental note to pick a bushel or two for Gordon one day if his mission proved successful. Yet thoughts of the little Bean cottage returned his mind to the business at hand, which it was long past time to address.

"How well do you know the caves and tunnels, Gordon?"

"Oh, like the back of my paw," replied the monster. "I've lived here my whole life, you see, and despite my debilitating nyctophobia, I have intimate knowledge of the caves' every nook and cranny."

"We are on a quest most perilous, you must understand," said Leek. "And it would be ever so helpful if you could show us to the exit."

"Gladly." Gordon smiled. "You have brought light where light has never shined before. And I will offer what aid I can, in payment for this boon."

Gordon then rose from the cavern floor, and his chest swelled to nearly the size of a zeppelin. The firefly family shone around his head, rejoicing in their expansive new domain, and the monster glowed with pleasure.

"Now follow me, into the dark," he said with obvious pride, "for I am not afraid."

The rabbits followed Gordon into the distance, hopping fifty of their longest hops to match his single stride. As they scrambled to keep up, Morel found herself sneaking curious glances at Leek. The rabbit bore no blade or bow, no shield or heavy club. Yet it had been he, not she, who had gotten them so far, and he had done so simply by giving. Leek had given Hamlin luck, which propelled them from the fish. His gift to King Kadogo had sprung from Hamlin's flute, which in turn had summoned the truffles. Gordon's gift now danced between his mighty horns, buzzing in cheery glee, and a pang of guilt seized Morel as she stared at her companion. It was Leek and his simple generosity that had carried them past the Great Ink and through the Jungle Prime Evil. Her spear, her sword, her mighty words of courage, had all proved sadly useless. As a guide, Morel had altogether failed.

Perhaps, thought Morel, she would try to be less rude. And maybe, if she was very lucky, she would yet prove her warrior's worth.

"It's not far now," said Gordon as he entered the largest of caverns. "The back door's just ahead."

But as he spoke, the cave floor trembled, and great stones came crashing from above. Gordon rushed to shield the rabbits with his bulk, and beneath this friendly canopy, the rabbits were quite safe. However, safety is a fleeting thing in Hat, and as the tremors came to a stop, Morel's hunter's sense sprang to high alert. She knew in an instant, beyond any semblance of doubt, that other hunters were near and that they were hunting rabbit.

Before she could cry out, the cavern walls shattered, and from them crawled a brand-new breed of Dimmer-Dammer designed only for destruction. The sharpened drills at their snouts revolved with sinister groans as they ground to a dusty pulp the rock that barred their way. Cold lights, affixed atop their iron heads, lit their warpath of doom. As the beasts converged upon their hapless prey, one such light trained its evil eye upon them. Its master rose behind it, and Gordon blanched in terror. For small as it was, this

was a beast of perfect blackness, cloaked in shadow everlasting, like the darkness he so feared. And from its mouth came even darker words.

"And so we meet again," said Millikin to Leek, licking a smudge of dust from his paw. "Never have I beheld this stinking pit of infamy, and yet, my eyes rejoice at the sight. It will make a fitting tomb for you and the wench."

Then Millikin turned his gaze to Gordon, whose great girth shivered in fright. Cats, and most animals in general, are quite adept at sensing fear—even when one tries very hard to hide it. But Millikin required no such sixth sense now. Gordon's fear was plain as day, a fact that made Millikin smirk.

"You fear me, monster, yes? You are right to do so, for I am he who walks unseen, the shadowmaster! It is I who command the blackness in your dreams, and it is I who rule the night! My stride brings with it ruin, and to cross your path, large as it may be, will bring me glory tenfold!"

But even as Gordon shrank in abject fear, the tiny she-rabbit, only a small fraction of his size, strode forward to defend him.

"Our host is not your business," spoke Morel, her

brown fur shimmering with fury. "Get thee gone, or you will rue the venomous words you so idly spit."

"My, my," hissed Millikin, "yet another empty threat from the mighty warrior princess. The toys that you call weapons may bring you passing comfort, but they cannot bring salvation."

Morel strode closer to Millikin's iron mole, and beneath its beam of light, her eyes sparkled with courage.

"You may not fear my sharpened steel or the paw that bears it. But you are wrong to doubt the rabbit in my charge, for he is the luck-giver! And no machine, no power you can muster, will ever quell his strength. If it is his hide you seek, then kindly come and try to take it. But first, you must pass me."

With that, Morel crouched low and readied herself to strike. But before the shield-maiden could leap, Gordon stepped between Morel and certain death.

"You are so brave for one so small," he told Morel. Gordon's dancing crown gleamed golden, in a sign of newfound courage. "And though my great breast may not boast as much against the dark, it does take hope. And in hope, surely there is courage."

"Well said, Gordon," whispered Leek. "As a matter

of fact, she gives me hope as well."

"I have my light," whispered Gordon to himself. And the black cats watched in sudden horror as he heaved himself to his full height, a colossus as of yore, and bellowed.

"I HAVE MY LIGHT! AND I . . . AM NOT . . . AFRAID!"

With that, Gordon breathed deep and roared. Dark green vapors shot from his gaping jaws, and as black cats leaped from their Dimmer-Dammers, the machines turned red, then white, and melted.

"Run, my friends!" commanded Gordon. "I will see to these intruders who dare invade my lair. For I am Gordon, and I am a monster! AND I . . . AM NOT . . . AFRAID!"

The rabbits sprang for the tunnel's exit, far in the distance, even as iron missiles whistled toward them through the air. Leek dodged two, then three, and yet even as he dodged and leaped, he did not forget his manners.

"Thank you, Gordon!" he yelped. "We will never forget you! And do have a look at the surface sometime! King Kadogo truly is a peach!"

Gordon was too busy to respond. The machines

swarmed his girth from every side, but in this, he was glad. For as he waded toward their leader, crushing the iron beasts with both his fists and feet, the fireflies grew ever brighter. Even they had risen to the defense of their new home, their bottoms shining fierce with patriotic ire. As Gordon towered over Millikin, whose hackles rose in fright, the monster's own huge shadow cast the black cat into darkness.

"Now, shadowmaster! Behold the shadow of true power, and tell me who's afraid!"

An answer never came. Millikin was already running back up the tunnel he himself had dug, his tail between his legs. He had never known such fear, he thought, and he dearly hoped his tail wouldn't stick permanently in such a position. Perhaps he'd have to have it surgically rearranged. Happiness, Millikin considered, was an increasingly evasive goal. And even as he ran, the black cat made a mental note to schedule a follow-up appointment with his therapist.

The caravan had stopped. Cecil listened carefully for some sign of their location or of Imbrolio, but the trunk was a thick one, and he heard nothing. Perhaps the villain had simply stopped to heed the call of nature, as Cecil rather needed to do himself. But by this time, Cecil had resigned both his spirit and stomach, as well as his bladder, to sacrifice in the name of adventure. So the boy crossed his legs, which helped, and continued to listen.

Long minutes passed before Cecil heard the so-called magician huffing and puffing as he climbed to the caravan's roof. The boy's heart froze in fear, for though a rough plan had been brewing in his head, it had not yet come to boil. Should Imbrolio find him now, surely all would be lost. Cecil clenched his fists and thought of Leek and prayed for just a little luck. If the trunk's lid opened now, he would need it.

The lid did not open, but Cecil heard the villain speak now clear as day—mere inches from his trunk.

"You're a crafty one indeed," said Imbrolio, "and your hiding place a good one. But I've found you in the end, as I always do. You may abandon hope of rescue or escape, and I suggest you have a nap, should your trembling relent. You must rest while you can, you see, for we have a show to perform!"

With that, Imbrolio let go a great cackle, which chilled the boy to his core. But the cackle quickly receded as Cecil heard the man climb down. The caravan grumbled back to life, and as it rolled on down the road, Cecil found just enough courage to crack the lid above him and peek out.

Tied to the caravan's roof, not two feet from his trunk, was a cage. And within its tiny confines was a rabbit, shivering in fear and grief. The rabbit paced its little prison and shook the bars with its paws, to no avail.

"Don't worry," Cecil whispered. "My name is Cecil Bean. I know now of the cats, and of the war you wage against them. So never fear, I will save you. I have the makings of a plan."

The rabbit's eyes grew wide, for it had thought its daily mission quite the secret. Conversation with a human was quite outside the rules, and rules, the rabbit considered, were important. All lucky rabbits had pledged sacred oaths to obey them.

The trunk then closed tight, and the rabbit calmed its nerves to try to think this through. Plans were all well and good when hatched by lucky rabbits. Saving the day was simply what they did. But since when did humans ever save the day for them? This was all highly irregular, thought the rabbit. Then again, being caught in a trap was highly irregular as well. The morning had been filled with high irregularity. And rather more was yet to come.

CHAPTER EIGHT

The path before them was a bleak one, barren and cruel. Leek and Morel had been walking for hours or days or even weeks. Both had quite lost track of time in their hunger and their thirst. Morel trudged doggedly forward, drawing from reserves of strength and will she never knew she had. Occasionally she turned, to be certain Leek still followed—and to her continued amazement, always he was there. But the sight of him broke her heart. Once almost chubby in his health, Leek's face was gaunt and sunken, his lustrous brown coat stained gray from the dust of the road. As to his cheery spirit, Leek seemed altogether listless and bent with the burden of certain defeat. Morel thought often that if she had but a single neep to give, she would force it on him. She would gladly go hungry herself if only Leek would smile, just once, however briefly.

"Let us pause," she croaked, "and rest."

Leek heard her voice, vaguely, as in a dream. And through the murk and haze, he saw her shape before him. But while every fiber of his body cried out for some small respite, his mind would not relent.

"We must press on," he mumbled, "for the sake of Cecil Bean."

"If you will not rest at my command," said Morel, "then rest for the sake of your boy. The hardest part lies before us, and we must save what strength remains. Come and lean against this rock. Do so for Cecil, and he will thank you for it when you see him."

Too tired to argue further, Leek's slim shoulders sank. The cold moon of Hat shone down from high above as if to mock his torment, and Leek collapsed to his knees to weep.

Morel stood above him, trying hard to hold her

great spear steady in case of sudden attack. She stared into the distance and resigned herself to sacrifice. She would give all, she knew, to see Leek meet his goal—even if it meant that she abandon hers. In this resolution, Morel discovered newfound strength. She realized she must harden herself further still, to the strength of steel itself. In her warrior's tongue, she spoke grim words.

"You must not weep, for we cannot spare the water."

Leek slowly raised his eyes to stare at his companion. Her will was greater than his own, he knew, and in that, he took small hope. Whenever one feels tired or weak or altogether helpless, it's nice to know one has a stalwart friend. Without exception, that always makes things at least a trifle better.

"Yes. Yes, of course, you're right." He sighed. "I will not weep again, unless it be with joy."

"See that you don't," said Morel, avoiding his gaze. "Our enemies do not cry, and we must become as hard as they or more so."

With that, Leek rose, and the pair crept on, two dusty specks on an endless plain of darkness. The faint path soon wound its way uphill, adding effort to their toil, and as the moon slid behind some wayward patch of cloud, Morel peered forward, into the distance, and swore beneath her breath.

"A storm approaches, it would seem," she whispered. "See how the blackness grows darker up ahead."

Leek raised his eyes to look, straining through the murk, and a cold wind blew hard against him, smiting what spirit remained.

"Yet even in this wind," he whispered, "the dark cloud does not move."

The cloud bank parted briefly, revealing the moon in pale and sudden brilliance, and in doing so, revealed what lay before them, stretching to the sky. There upon a crooked mountain sat a sprawling compound, evil beyond measure. This was the fortress of the cats, and it had no name but doom. This was the seat of all bad luck's grim power, a power so great within the world of Hat that it seeps into our own. Here at night, when humans fall asleep, their black cats come to plot dark new twists of fate. Here they conspire and compare wicked notes and laugh at all that is good. Here, with iron chalices, they toast to chaos, to sadness and despair. And here they curse the rabbits and all who would stand with them. Here

no hope may rise. There rose only one great tower, so tall as to nearly kiss the moon itself. This, Leek knew, was the one great goal he sought. For within, it was said, he might find some means of reunion with his boy.

Leek looked up at the castle and sighed at the challenge ahead. This was the home of the Dimmer-Dammers, and against those sinister engines, steaming with hate for his kind, what chance had two small rabbits—and one unarmed at that? Leek wished he had some weapon, some token of defense, but wishes are not granted on the mountain of ill luck. Unless, thought Leek with a grimace, one wishes for defeat.

"This does seem a frightfully intimidating prospect," he said, and sighed, "yet of course I've still got to try. But Morel, I think it best you now turn tail and hop back home. Here there's just no hope, even for mighty warriors like you wielding great swords and spears. You should really go back to Komatsuna, much as I hate to say it. I'd feel just terrible if you were hurt. Please go back while I press forward alone."

Morel turned to stare at Leek, her sole companion in this forsaken land, and laughed.

"Return? Return to what? To tears? To heart-ache? To the bitter taste of neeps? Nay, Leek, you will not see me off this day. For never has a rabbit come so far along the hopeless road, against all odds, to behold at last its end. Together we shall walk, as we long have done, and together, we shall storm the palace gates. I too sense the danger. It is clear enough to see. Yet even should we fail, I am certain glory awaits."

"Small consolation, but consolation nonetheless, I suppose," said Leek, who had never won an argument with Morel—even when he was pretty sure he was right. "But I'll take it. All right, glory it is. And we will seek it together, until our last remaining breath. Proceed."

But Morel had already proceeded, as was her way, and Leek hopped very quickly to catch up with her, even as she made for the shadow ahead.

The path rose steep and high, and as the pair crept slowly toward its zenith, the rock converged on either side. Soon, they could no longer walk abreast, and Morel stepped quickly to the lead, her spear held ever at the ready.

"Strange," whispered Morel, "that the path should

go unguarded. The cats are far too lax in their defense."

Leek smiled. "Well, they haven't much to fear in one small rabbit and his guide."

Morel scanned the ramparts looming ahead, in search of feline sentries, but there were none to see. The quiet that enveloped them was absolute, and Morel awaited with dread the hiss or cry that must surely break it—and summon the cats to arms. But no call came, shrill and piercing in the night, as the companions marched on to whatever lay ahead.

Then, as one, the rabbits beheld the very last thing they had ever expected to behold.

It was a turnip.

There, where even thorn and vine had never thought to grow, was a turnip, just sitting in the dirt. What's more, it was a specimen of the very highest quality, a fact Morel's sad stomach hastened to confirm.

"A turnip!" she gasped. "Here beyond the reach of hope, far from the world that has a sun, luck has provided, in defiance of the cats! With this turnip, this gift of the ancient fates, we will fortify ourselves for battle! And with the strength that it provides, we will scale the castle walls! None shall stand against us!"

With that, Morel rushed forward. But Leek paused, uncertain, and sniffed at the turnip ahead, which just didn't smell quite right. It had been some time since he had smelled one, and yet in his long, strange travels, Leek had learned a thing or two. What's more, he'd learned the hard way.

And as Leek recalled the last turnip that had presented itself to him, so bawdy and so fine, he sprang to the she-rabbit's side.

"Wait! Morel! This turnip is a trap!"

But the trap had already sprung. Rising from the earth around them, with speed the naked eye could scarcely catch, came a mammoth paw of iron. As it emerged, its talons sprang forth, like the claws of some great cat, and snapped shut together at their tips. Leek could only rush to the rigid bars before him and peer out as the cage ascended into the air, pushed from beneath by a mighty iron arm. And as he stared, in shock and deep regret, the cage rose to the height of the fortress walls, where dark legions came forth to greet them.

At their head was Millikin.

"I really should have thought of this sooner." The

cat grinned. "What a bad little kitty I've been. To think we've been after you all this time, and what finally puts an end to your ridiculous quest is a common turnip. It boggles the mind! But it's all gone right in the long run, or tragically wrong, depending on your perspective, and that's what counts."

"What happens now?" snarled Leek.

"Now?" Millikin smiled. "Oh, you'll be delighted to know I've arranged some very cozy quarters for you two in the pit of our darkest dungeon. And while you rot, for the rest of time and beyond, I'll be busy crossing Cecil's path. I plan to begin directly after brunch, in fact. My boy and I have quite a bit of catching up to do."

"He isn't yours!" screamed Leek. "He's my boy! The human Bean is mine and mine alone!"

"Not anymore," said Millikin. And with that, he turned away, his sinister tail swishing to and fro in glee. Millikin giggled to himself. At this rate, he'd be happy in no time. With Leek defeated and imprisoned, nothing would stand in his way. And if a little boy's lifelong misfortune couldn't make him happy, what else possibly could?

Cecil raised the lid of the trunk and peered out. He wasn't quite sure whether he liked what he saw or not. This was no tidy village. This was the Great Big City. Loud motorcars whizzed by, blaring their horns in rage at who-knows-what. Street vendors strode amid the crowd, hawking various foodstuffs that, to Cecil, didn't seem fit to eat.

For his part, Imbrolio was tremendously busy, making preparations for his show. Imbrolio loved the Great Big City, mainly because he never felt alone there. In tiny country villages, you see, Imbrolio's dishonesty stood out, at least to him, like an enormous throbbing sore thumb. But in the Great Big City, dishonesty ran rampant, and that made Imbrolio happy, since it made him feel less bad. Misery loves company, as the saying goes, and villainy adores it.

As Imbrolio bustled about, assembling his rickety stage and stuffing colored scarves down his pants, he whistled a sinister tune. And so deep was his happy reverie that Imbrolio failed to notice entirely as a small boy emerged from the trunk atop his caravan, slipped down its side, and melted into the hubbub.

"This," said the charlatan to himself, "will be a show to remember."

Morel strained at the iron lattice before her and cursed a dark blue streak. Her sword and spear stripped from her desperate paws, the rabbits would now be held captive, forever and ever and then some. At Morel's back and sides were walls of heavy granite, ten feet thick or more, and she knew the gate would have to age and rust and rot away before she might hope for escape. They'd never last that long, she thought, even on full stomachs. And so she turned to Leek, in hope of seeing his smile.

Leek was asleep in the corner, curled up like a tiny croissant. His fur was filthy and matted, and even in his slumber, he whimpered in defeat. They had come so far, so very far, only to be beaten. Morel sighed. She hadn't even had a chance to fight, and in that, she once again felt useless.

But Morel had one weapon left, which no cat could ever take away. It was now almost forgotten, unused as it long had been. Yet even in their darkest hour, Morel recalled the words she had spoken in the

land of snow and ice. She now remembered well her promise: "We will give each other luck."

Morel strode slow and soft to her companion and knelt by his tiny side.

"Leek, dear Leek," she whispered, "oft have I watched, with spear in paw, as you have given luck to others and sought nothing in return. And as I have borne witness to your small brand of courage, I have done naught but roll my eyes. Now, dear Leek, you must not give but take. If any luck remains within my warrior's heart, I now offer it to you."

Morel reached out and gently brushed Leek's forehead with her paw—just as long ago she had often brushed against her girl. Leek murmured in his sleep, and even in the dark, his face grew calm and came alight with a glow. For deep within his slumber, a song began to sound.

The melody reached deep inside him. There, in the hidden valleys of his soul, it discovered all the secret things that made him sad and banished them forever. Leek felt that he was floating, and his body tingled from the tips of his whiskers to the end of his cotton-ball tail. Leek hoped the song would never stop.

Then he sat bolt upright and smiled.

"Hamlin!"

"This," came a voice from behind them, "is all a terrible mistake."

The rabbits turned, and there stood Hamlin, grinning. In his paw was his faithful flute, and on his back was slung a potbelly bow and a quiver of gray arrows.

"Hamlin!" cried Morel. "Most noble of mice! The sight of you is welcome, as is the sound of your song! But how is it, in the name of all good luck, that we now come to hear it?"

"Well," said the mouse, "it wasn't easy. There I sat, amid Kadogo and his tribe, as they sang your funeral dirge. Quite a depressing tune, I can assure you, and I had to cover my ears, for fear of sorrow—and subsequent dehydration. But then along came Gordon to assure us you yet lived."

"Gordon!" gasped Morel. "He saved us in the caves."

"Oh yes." Hamlin smiled. "He told us all about it. Though to hear him tell the tale, it was you two who saved him. He's terribly grateful, you know. And so he led me through the caves and showed me his back door. There I found your tracks, which I've been tracking ever since. I've become quite a remarkable tracker, you know, for a minstrel."

"But how did you ever pass the Dimmer-Dammers and find us in our prison?" exclaimed the she-rabbit in ever-mounting wonder.

"I rode in on one." Hamlin grinned. "In secret—and, I might add, relative comfort."

"How clever!" said Leek, in admiration of the mouse.

"Well, I shouldn't like to brag," said Hamlin. "And besides, there isn't time. Now then. I've borrowed the key, and Morel, I've brought your weapons. So you just take them and make for the tower and return to the world that has a sun. Perhaps we'll meet again one day, and only then will we speak at length of our collective cleverness."

With that, Hamlin turned to go.

"But Hamlin!" cried Morel, fitting the great key to its lock, "wherever are you going?"

"To play a game," came the response. "A game of cat and mouse."

CHAPTER NINE

The cats were all very busy clapping Millikin on the back when the mouse went sprinting by. For a moment, all were struck quite dumb, as no mouse had ever walked the confines of their fortress, let alone a mouse so rude.

"Losers!" sang out Hamlin, even as he ran. "Eat my dust! That's all the taste you'll have of me this day!"

Then their instincts kicked in, turbocharged with rage. A thousand cats scrambled instantly after the mouse, while ten thousand more sprang for their various weapons. Still more leaped to the Dimmer-Dammers, which immediately rumbled to life. And as the ebony army chased after little Hamlin, Millikin was left alone. For much as he would have liked to chase the mouse himself, you see, a stronger instinct forbade it. That instinct was fear.

So, fingering the hilt of his rapier, Millikin turned from the chase and strode instead for the tower.

The rabbits emerged from the depths to behold a courtyard of fine black stone. Morel peeked, noiseless, from shadow as the tower guards abandoned their posts, leaving them quite unguarded. To the spire's iron door, Morel guessed, was a sprint of some three hundred yards. Tired as they were, she was certain they could reach it.

"Can you run?" she asked Leek.

"I've never felt faster," came the staunch reply, "for only speed will help me reach my boy. But we can't abandon Hamlin to the talons of the cats!"

"Hamlin has grown wise in the warrior's way," said Morel, "and we must now honor his courage, for such was his last wish.

"And besides," she added with a grin, "maybe he'll get lucky."

"Then let us run," said Leek, "to the tower and our humans beyond."

And so they ran, two dusty blurs across a court of pure, pitch black. But even as they neared the mammoth door before them, and certain escape within, the realm of Hat laughed yet again, pitiless and cold. For Hamlin, brave as he was, was but a stranger to these grounds. As the mouse careened throughout the fort's broad roads and narrow alleys, he took a wayward turn, which led back to whence he'd come. To his horror, Hamlin spied his friends, for whom he had braved all. As he skittered to a stop, in grim shock at what he'd done, the cats pulled up behind him. They too saw the rabbits, and when they did, their taste for mouse was quickly cast aside. Never had their sacred monolith been breached by those unworthy of its secrets. And as one, the cats arose, a teeming, writhing mass that hissed with hate as it surged forward to attack.

"Hurry!" cried Leek. "We can beat them yet and bar the door behind!"

Morel did not hurry, or even listen, but paused to

gaze at the black tide roaring toward her. This was the foe from which she long had hidden. This was the foe that had suppressed her kind, and in turn her human, the girl Morel so missed. This force, she knew, now sought to bring her ruin, and perhaps it would bring just that. But she would not share such a fate with Leek, for this was her moment, of which her tribe might sing.

"Go," she said, even as Leek pried the doors apart. "Go and find your boy. Bring him fair luck for as long as he should live. When he sleeps and you rest in your own hole, then think of me, the she-rabbit who loved you."

"What!" yelped Leek. "Never! Never without you, Morel!"

"Take this," said Morel, handing Leek her sword, "and GO!"

With that, Morel kicked Leek hard in the chest with her mighty hind leg. And as he sailed through that great arch, where no rabbit had ever gone before, she reached forward, against her every wish, and drew the doors shut with a fateful clang. In the silence that ensued, she closed her eyes and whispered softly to her spear.

"And now, great spear, old friend, at last our time has come."

Morel turned slowly to face the army of cats bearing down. She voiced no threat or words of courage. As she leaped to attack, she simply grinned, for she had not proved useless.

Leek blinked and blinked again as his eyes adjusted to the light, or lack thereof. As soon as he had caught his breath, which Morel had quite knocked away, he leaped to his feet and, in panic, sought the door. But where some knob or handle should have been to help him, there was only iron, smooth and cold to the touch. In deep dismay, he turned to stare agape.

The citadel rose infinite above him, a cylinder without end, stretching to the sky. Lining its walls, spaced only inches apart, were innumerable hatches, wrought carefully of iron and marked with curious signs, as if scratched there by some craftsman's sharpened claw. On each hatch, too, there was an iron ring, which one might turn should one wish to enter.

"Portals," gasped Leek in sudden wonder. "These must be portals to the world that has a sun. But which one, of all these many paths, will lead to Cecil Bean?"

Praying his luck would hold for just one moment more, Leek thus strode to the nearest hatch. There he found that its ring swiveled lightly on its mooring, and the hatch popped promptly open, with a snort and a hiss of hot steam.

"I hereby do honor, with humble thanks and deep humility, to Hamlin, the minstrel mouse," spoke Leek in solemn voice, "and to Morel, mightiest of all rabbits trapped in the world of Hat, and the one that I love most in this world or any other. May my human boy await."

Leek peeped into the hatch. Before his feet had even thought to follow, his head had emerged from a storm drain. Looking about, he saw a great many humans, but these were humans the likes of which he'd never seen before. The men all wore felt hats with little feathers at their sides and short leather shorts suspended by matching suspenders. The women seemed comprised primarily of ruddy cheeks and jowls, which shook with laughter and song. All held great flagons brimming with bubbling froth, and several merry souls swayed and stumbled as they danced.

As Leek stared upward in confusion, he caught

the gaze of a sparrow perched at the shindig's edge.

"*Guten tag!*" it chirped.

Leek retreated at once and promptly shut the hatch, sealing it tight with a twist.

"Well," said the rabbit with a sigh, staring up at the countless hatches above, "it must be here somewhere. I suppose I should try one more and then another. The third time's usually the charm."

"You will find no charm within my tower," came a voice, "the third time or any other."

It was Millikin. And as he strode forward from shadow, his rapier glistened and gleamed.

"No rabbit has ever beheld what you now see before you," he sneered. "And by all that is dark and unholy, I swear you shall be the last."

But while Millikin was really quite certain that Leek would tremble in fear and that his blood would run cold in his veins and that he would scarcely have time to beg for mercy before meeting his untimely end (a circumstance that seemed to Millikin entirely overdue), that's not what happened at all. On the contrary, Leek got mad. And as he held the sword of Morel before him, he spoke with surprising conviction.

"Rapscallion," he said. "Long have we vied, in this world and the other, for the fate of Cecil Bean. But I have grown weary, in my long travels, of idle talk and banter. Now I, Leek, the luck-giver, make this fell decree, with only my foe to bear witness. Tonight, our battle ends. And before you fall, know this: never again, in all the days that follow, shall my boy ever step in dog poop!

"Have at thee!" he added in passion.

"With pleasure," hissed Millikin. At that, their swords flashed as one and met with an epic ring.

Quite the crowd stood waiting. As they peered and pointed at the ramshackle caravan, even the savvy city-folk murmured in great anticipation of the magical wonders to come. They had their business affairs and their politics to consider, and almost everyone assembled considered themselves terribly and irrevocably important, in one way or another. But with the promise of magic to come, all that was put on hold. Everyone loves magic, you see—even very important businessmen.

In their midst stood Cecil Bean, a simple country lad perhaps, but an adventurer as well. And Cecil had bigger things to consider than Imbrolio's cheap parlor tricks and chicanery, for the boy had a riddle to solve. Two riddles, really, but the one that weighed more heavily on Cecil was the matter of bad luck—and precisely how to avoid it. The mysterious gentleman had done it, and his cat had up and quit. But why?

As Cecil thought and thought, his stomach chose to whine. It hadn't had a bite in ages, after all, and could hardly be blamed for complaining. But even as Cecil's tummy cried out in mutinous tones, his nose caught the scent of hot scone.

"Fresh scones!" cried a shriveled old woman, carrying her basket before her. "Fresh scones, piping hot, the finest in the land!"

Cecil, betrayed by both his stomach and his sniffer, couldn't help but look, and lock eyes with the shrunken hag.

"Fresh scone, my boy?" asked the woman, who had just the hint of a beard.

"No thank you," said the boy. "I haven't any money, I'm afraid, though they do smell quite delicious."

"Delicious? Why, these are the finest scones that a boy could ever buy, and if I'm not mistaken, I suppose you wonder why. Just what might it be, you ask, that makes my scones so fine? That, dear boy, is a secret, and the answer's purely mine."

"Well," said Cecil sadly, much to the disappointment of his stomach, "I suppose the point is moot, since I am too poor to buy one."

"Ah, but you may have one free of charge," said the woman with a genuine smile, "with kind regards to your stomach. And you may have the secret, too, for what it's worth."

"Thank you!" said Cecil as he commenced to munch on his scone. Truly, it was the very finest scone on which he'd ever munched.

"I make them myself, from scratch," whispered the woman, with a wink from her one good eye. With that, she hobbled away and soon disappeared in the crowd.

Not much of a secret, considered Cecil as he munched.

Then, in a sudden flash, the boy's eyes widened in abject revelation. His mouth agape, a single crumb of scone fell to the concrete below. And just at his most desperate hour, Cecil Bean experienced a moment of startling clarity:

He would have to make his own luck, all by himself, from scratch.

The duel raged on within the confines of the tower, and Millikin had to admit, the pair were evenly matched. Though Millikin was larger and well-schooled in the arts of war, Leek's passion was no small one. Though his sword swung wildly, with little discipline or skill, it nonetheless swung hard. Leek sought to smite the black cat time and time again, and Millikin could only dodge and parry and leap from the ladders and railings that lined the tower walls. Leek did not dodge or parry. He only advanced, crying his battle cry.

"For Bean, for Bean!" he bellowed.

As it slowly dawned on Millikin that he required some advantage, and preferably an unfair one, he hugged the tower wall and turned an iron ring behind him. As Leek came sprinting toward his foe, Millikin hissed and stepped into the portal, the rabbit just behind.

The pair came tumbling from a ventilation shaft, only to land atop a speeding locomotive, far beneath the streets of some metropolis. As the wind whistled between them, Millikin grinned.

"Our battle now ranges beyond the realm of shadow! And I, with my claws and my sure footing, am sure to prove the victor!"

"Yet a rabbit's feet are lucky," snarled Leek, swinging his sword, "and whichever world you seek in which to fight, it matters not! For you shall have your comeuppance!"

But before he could receive his due comeuppance, Millikin leaped from the train into a crack in the tunnel wall. Leek hopped after in hot pursuit, only to find himself popping from a portal back in the tower of the cats. Millikin was just twisting the ring on yet another hatch and stepping in. But Leek's speed was that of light itself, and he swung at Millikin's tail as he came, carving a tuft of black fur.

The pair rolled like a ball across an icy path piled high with snow, snarling and biting as they did. A passing team of huskies was caught quite unawares, as was their Inuit master, by the epic duel that appeared as if from the very ether before them. But even as the huskies gathered their wits and lunged forward with twelve great woofs, the pugilists rolled straight into a snowbank and passed back into Hat.

Millikin leaped into another hatch, Leek just

inches behind, and dropped into a factory, where he swung around to face his foe. As the two paced and parried along a black conveyor belt, great blades and hammers descended from above. Millikin stepped to a side, dodging a ten-ton press, and lunged at Leek, who slipped and fell. But before the press could flatten him, Leek rolled to his left and dropped into a pail. Millikin leaped after, for the pail, too, was a portal.

Now it was Leek who turned an iron ring and hopped into the hole behind. As rain washed down in torrents, the pair emerged amid the rigging of a ship, which spun like a top at the whim of an angry sea.

"My father was a pirate!" screamed Millikin over the storm. "And today I do him honor!"

"I'll trim your black beard with my blade!" squealed Leek, swinging from a rope and holding his sword with his teeth. But before Millikin could concoct some suitable retort, his foe had dropped into a dinghy, returning to the tower beyond.

Millikin shook the rain from his black mane as he tumbled back into Hat and, springing to his feet, chased Leek into yet another hatch. But there Leek dropped his sword and hoisted a stout staff instead.

The black cat eyed the room's thin walls made of fine white paper and grasped a pair of nunchucks, which he swung with grim abandon.

"I am the seven-hundred-and-seventy-seventh son of a seven-hundred-and-seventy-seventh son," said Leek, bringing his staff to rest on Millikin's head with a satisfying smack. "My family line has always sought to multiply, and I am their great product!"

"And yet today," scowled Millikin, "I will teach a lesson in division when I cleave your body from its head."

With that, the cat reclaimed his sword and slipped beneath a basket. Leek grasped his sword again and leaped after Millikin in hot pursuit.

An elderly woman had just removed her tea cozy from a pot of hot sassafras tea. She had tuned her small transistor to a particularly soothing station, which offered easy listening, and removed her inch-thick spectacles to simply pause and relax. But to her ears came not the subtle croons for which she'd hoped, but cries of great calamity, the clash of steel on steel. A blur of writhing fur streaked past her pink recliner, and rushing to replace her glasses on their perch, the woman sat bolt upright in alarm. But as quickly as it had come, the blur vanished, gone with a flash behind the davenport. At length, the woman dared to breathe again and, at last, to sip her tea. She had always maintained grave suspicions about that davenport, though primarily from an aesthetic perspective, and resolved to banish it promptly to the garage.

The next hatch offered little opportunity for battle. Black cat and dusty rabbit spilled forth into a street as a hundred men came rushing by wearing bright red kerchiefs around their necks. As Leek and Millikin turned to spy the cause of their great haste, the ground shook with a fury that nearly matched their own. A bovine stampede descended upon them, and the pair careened betwixt the hooves of snorting bulls, which ran amok in pursuit of those crimson scarves. Millikin and his foe leaped together to the safety of a barrel and passed silently back into Hat.

Millikin breathed heavy within the tower of the cats, and Leek leaned exhausted on his sword.

"Just give me a moment," rasped the cat, "and I will give thee respite. For once I've caught my breath, I will bestow upon you slumber without end."

"Whenever you're ready," said Leek, gasping for

breath, "I await, with blade in paw. But before you strike again, black shadow, you must ask yourself one question—and think long before you answer."

Millikin narrowed his eyes as Leek reached behind his ball of tail, turned an iron ring, and whispered.

"Do I feel lucky?"

Even as the hatch popped open, Millikin sprang, holding his sword before him. But as that mighty blow neared Leek, the rabbit stepped aside. Millikin flew past him, into the waiting maw of the hatch, and little Leek reached out, brushing the black fur with his paw—just as he had always brushed the hem of Cecil's trousers.

As the tip of Millikin's tail disappeared into the hole, Leek smiled and sealed the hatch behind it.

"Best of luck, old foe," he said. "And may we never meet again."

Millikin tumbled from a hang glider's backpack, cursing and spitting and hissing with rage at his opponent's loathsome trick. Trickery was his expertise, not Leek's, and the black cat howled as he fell, desperate to return from whence he'd come. A thatched roof appeared all too soon below him, and Millikin clawed at the air to no avail, then tumbled through with a crash.

PLOP.

Millikin paused to collect himself and sniff the air. Fragrant embers smoldered nearby in a hearth, and the soothing scent brought sudden calm to Millikin's wrath. His eyes drifted to a rough-hewn table piled high with rods and netting, and at length the black cat slowly turned, to find himself perched on a lap.

The old man, to whom the lap belonged, regarded the cat at length.

Millikin had stumbled into the remote and invitingly rustic abode of an elderly Canadian bachelor who, after some forty-odd years working a drill press, had resolved to spend his retirement strolling the Northern backcountry in pursuit of rainbow trout.

"Well, this is a bit of unexpected luck," said the man, smiling. "I could use some company."

The man slowly extended a hand, from which Millikin initially shrank. In all his years, he'd always avoided human detection and, above all, actual contact. But as the hand approached, Millikin felt somehow drawn—and raised himself to meet it, noting its every detail. Calloused from toil, but strong and clean, still laced with the slightest scent of the stream. And then, for the very first time in his life, Millikin found his ears gently scratched, from just behind, in just that spot.

Ecstasy.

As the old man scratched away, he thanked goodness for a newfound friend. As for Millikin, all thoughts of battle, of dark towers and bad luck, melted from his heart. And as that heart grew fast less black and filled with the rosy glow of simple satisfaction, even the memory of a boy named Cecil Bean soon faded and dissolved, forever. He had a new human now. And in that he was . . . *happy.*

"I suppose you'd like a bite of fresh trout." The man grinned.

And as Millikin plodded softly to the bowl that would always be his, he sighed in deep thanksgiving. Now *this* was therapeutic.

CHAPTER TEN

Leek gazed up at the tower's dizzying height, and at the infinite portals that lined its every inch. Behind one awaited his human as well as his hole near Cecil's house. It might take years, or even the rest of his life, to plumb the depths of every hatch. But to this fate the rabbit was resigned.

Until he heard again the fearsome sound of battle.

As Leek perked up his ears, which fought against the thickness of the tower's iron walls, he heard the clash of some small blade on metal, and with that, he remembered Morel.

Morel, who would give all for his sake, and the sake of Leek's small boy. Morel, whose small pink nose oft wrinkled in such a winsome way. Morel, who even now faced death for the one she'd come to love.

I cannot go to Cecil, thought Leek, and look him in the eye. Not without Morel, now knowing that she loves me. For while my boy will always be my pride, my duty, and my very finest friend, Morel is something more. And any luck I might bestow on Cecil, however freely given, would be hollow without her at my side.

"No," he said aloud. "I will not go to Cecil, or the world that has a sun, without Morel."

The tower doors burst open then, with the force of a falling hulk. The Dimmer-Dammer spun once, wobbled woozily on its feet, and with one last mammoth fart of steam, collapsed with a crash that sent its pilot sprawling. Moonlight poured into the tower, cold and pale as ever, and with that, Leek strode out, to stand beneath its source.

The carnage of war awaited. A thousand lifeless Dimmer-Dammers lay strewn haphazard in death, their iron corpses dull and charred, while ten thousand cats limped within their shadows, moaning and licking their wounds. And yet more came, fresh and furious with rage, thirsting for vengeance on the two small souls standing weary yet defiant before the tower door.

Hamlin bent his bow to fire his last arrow and cursed the quiver that could not bear another. At his side stood Morel, shield-maiden of the clan of Komatsuna, her eyes still bright with pride and shining fierce in glory. Her great spear notched and pitted in proof of her great deeds, Morel still stood her ground and beckoned the cats to come.

"Come forth, black legions! Come forth and taste my blade! For until its strength is broken, you will never have my Leek! He hastens even now unto another world, and there, beneath the sun, no war machine may follow!"

"And yet your Leek is here," spoke the voice behind her, "to stand with his Morel."

Morel turned slowly yet surely to gaze upon small Leek. And though in the past, her eyes had rolled when he sought to disobey, a tear rolled now instead and wet her longest whisker.

"We cannot stand much longer," she said. "But

we will stand together, this fellowship of three, till we can stand no more."

"My name," said the Great Imbrolio, "is the Great Imbrolio. And I am a famous magician."

"Capital!" bellowed the crowd. "Hooray for magic and its mysteries!"

"And now," hissed the Great Imbrolio, "on with the show!"

Of course, the show was anything but magical. On the contrary, it remained quite amateur and transparent. His deck of cards was still quite clearly stacked, and the length of colorful scarves he withdrew from his fist smelled ever so faintly of pee. Long before the Great Imbrolio had even gotten to his best material, the crowd began to protest.

"Fraud!"

"Charlatan!"

"Swindler!"

"Cheat!"

"Pee-pants!"

But the Great Imbrolio had heard it all before, and he knew what would quiet the crowd. He'd give the fools their precious magic.

"Silence!"

Something in the man's voice was so absolutely chilling, even the most important of businessmen decided they'd better just relax and save their rude remarks for the ambivalent hipsters who'd collectively annexed their coffee shops.

"For my final trick, I will require a volunteer from the audience."

Before anyone could even think to raise a hand, Cecil Bean strode forward and leaped upon the stage. Though the Great Imbrolio thought the boy seemed vaguely familiar, he could not place his face. So he paused and grinned, in hope of dramatic effect, and handed him his hat.

"Well, now, my overzealous friend! I have a question to pose. Would you say, boy, that this hat is an absolutely normal hat? Would you say that you have never inspected a more normal hat in all your life?"

"No," said Cecil Bean. "And I am not your friend."

"No?" demanded the Great Imbrolio. "No? Then I suppose you'd also dare to say that THIS is not a normal rabbit!"

With that, the man brought forth the rabbit from beneath his tattered cloak, holding it by the ears. The rabbit did not know quite what to expect. This was all highly irregular, as far as it was concerned.

"I must make my own luck now," whispered Cecil to himself. And as he peered down into the hat and beheld its bright red lining, he pondered the second riddle—and the matter of rabbit extraction.

"The answers to even the greatest of secrets are often right before us, if we only choose to look." That's what the mysterious gentleman had said. So Cecil looked right before him as instructed, and the boy did notice something he hadn't quite noticed before.

It was a label, pressed deep in the hat's red lining by some old-fashioned sort of stamp (the sort employed by only the finest of hatters). In brilliant scripted letters of pure and glittering gold, it read as such:

Cecil stared at the letters. Imbrolio stared at Cecil. The crowd stared at them both, waiting for something to happen.

Then Cecil cried out, in a voice that rose clear and true above the passing motorcars, and echoed in Imbrolio's ears forever.

"McHATTIE!"

Leek lowered his sword, and his jaw dropped shortly after. Hamlin's eyes grew wide, and Morel cried out in wonder. Even the Dimmer-Dammers paused in their assault as the black army raised its green eyes to the sky.

A tempest was upon them.

Stretching vast and tall, taller than even the tower, came the storm, which screamed and spun like a dervish. But as it came ever closer, it carved no swath of destruction, as tempests usually do. No, as it came, it left no trail of waste. It consumed no root or rock. Yet as Leek stood transfixed and gazed into its eye, he could swear he saw small shapes tossed about within.

Only when the storm crept over the fortress wall, and snatched up the companions, did Leek learn what the shapes were.

They were rabbits. And precisely six seconds later . . .

The rabbits came spouting from the hat like a geyser. First one, then another, and then the full five hundred of Komatsuna's clan came bursting forth into the air, to bask in the warmth of the world that has a sun. And when the last of the rabbits had finally trickled out, it was followed, rather anticlimactically, by one small mouse, bearing a flute.

The crowd didn't quite know what to make of that.

As Imbrolio stared at Cecil, and at the horde of rabbit warriors assembling at his back, he promptly recalled his dream. He immediately dropped the rabbit from his hand, in a state of shock and awe. Two particularly menacing rabbits stepped forward to stand at Cecil's side. One brandished a gruesome spear. And the Great Imbrolio, charlatan and fraud, immediately wet his pants, for the second soggy time in one single week.

"And now for my final trick," said Cecil Bean, staring hard at Imbrolio with a penetrating gaze. "Disappear."

Imbrolio needed no encouragement. And he ran

as he had never run before, to hide from the awful warriors and the conjurer who had summoned them. Imbrolio ran across three counties until he reached the sea. There he ran straight up a gangplank and onto a freighter, which promptly sailed for Patagonia, where Imbrolio still lives, in fear of rabbits and of magic. But thanks to Cecil Bean, he did discover his true calling and now owns a small but successful diaper-cleaning service, which happens to be environmentally friendly. So you see, even peeing one's pants can be a lucky thing from time to time. In Imbrolio's case, it was the only real job experience he had.

Cecil turned to the crowd, which stared aghast. Now *that* was a magic trick. And from far back within their masses, a single set of hands began to clap.

"Bravo," said the mysterious gentleman who once had owned the hat. As he clapped, he strode forward through the crowd, which now cheered in abject rapture, to shake the boy's small hand.

"Finest magic I've seen in many years," he said to Cecil. "You're a quick study, young man, and will no doubt make a very fine magician. I daresay you'll look quite dapper in my hat."

"Thank you, sir," said Cecil, blushing slightly.

"Now tell me, please," said the mysterious gentleman, "whatever will a boy like you do next?"

"That, sir," said Cecil Bean, "is a secret."

"Quite right," said the mysterious gentleman. "You're learning."

And with that, the gentleman disappeared in a burst of purple smoke.

Cecil then turned to find one particular rabbit, which leaped into his arms and wept in perfect joy. Leek had found his boy at last, and he rubbed his paws all over him, for all the time he'd lost. But as the pair embraced, he paused at Cecil's whisper.

"You'd be so proud of me. I made my own luck, all by myself, from scratch."

Leek leaned back in Cecil's arms, and dread crept through him as he stared up at the boy. If his human could make his own luck, he'd have little use for Leek.

"But I think we'll be better as a team." Cecil smiled. "You watch my back, and I'll watch yours—forever."

Leek considered such a prospect. He had never had a lucky human before.

It didn't sound half bad.

The tribe of King Kadogo rustled and bustled about, preparing a warm bed of coals. On state occasions, you see, truffles like to toast themselves a bit prior to being eaten. This was precisely such a time. For the chief had ordered that a great feast be held in Gordon's honor and that it take place on the beach, on the shores of the Great Ink.

The potbellies had all lit torches, and the truffles scampered about in the absolute highest of spirits. Soon enough, Gordon lumbered out of the jungle, his crown of little fireflies shining with golden glee. A thousand toasted truffles ran scampering in his direction and leaped promptly into his jaws. The truffles considered it a wonderful thing to be eaten by Gordon, as his bowels produced a very potent brand of fertilizer, which was certified organic. Gordon, for his part, was delighted to oblige.

As the potbellies danced and the fireflies shone and the truffles cozied up in the coals, Gordon and Kadogo stared out at the great black sea, which sparkled beneath the moon. And as they sat and pondered, and discussed the mysteries of Hat, they wondered what had become of lucky Leek and brave Morel. But before they could agree on the fate of the rabbits and their mouse, a voice came gurgling from the water.

"I say," said the sea monster, "is this a truffle roast?"

"It is indeed!" said King Kadogo. "And you are most welcome to join us, should the truffle herd prove willing!"

"Why, I'd be delighted to eat something, anything in fact," said the fish, "so long as it isn't neeps."

The other rabbits had all returned to their various humans. It wasn't long before only Leek, Morel, and Hamlin trailed Cecil through the meadows as he made his way back home to his cottage on the hill. Leek knew that soon enough the fellowship of three would sunder and only he would remain. Morel had her girl to consider, and she could not tarry long— such was her duty. Leek could hardly object.

"I know, Morel," said he, "that soon our paths

must part, and that you must seek your girl."

"She lies ahead," replied Morel, "and indeed, to give her luck will make me glad. She waits for me in a village, where she lives in a fourth-floor flat."

"Now wait just a moment," said Leek, hope rising in his heart. "I don't suppose your girl likes watermelon chewing gum?"

"She does indeed," said Morel, raising an eyebrow in question. "Oft have I dreamed of her sitting near the balcony. And always have I known that as she pined for brighter days and happy twists of fate, she would no doubt chew her gum as she awaited my return."

"Well," said Leek, "now isn't that lucky!"

So it was that the rabbits returned to the village of their youth, and watched with shining eyes as Cecil made a friend. This friend had, long ago, tossed gum in Cecil's hair. Still, she couldn't help but admire the cut of Cecil's jib (which is a five-dollar way of saying she liked him), and in future days, it would make the rabbits happy to follow, paw in paw, as their humans strolled together, hand in hand. The only casualty of the romance, so far as anyone could tell, was that the girl was forced to abandon watermelon chewing gum, given that it made Cecil sneeze. She now chews grape exclusively.

At the end of their long journey, which came welcome to all concerned, the rabbits' time to rest arrived at last. But before they took to bed, Hamlin said farewell.

"My friends, dear rabbits." He sighed as he shouldered his flute. "A wandering minstrel wanders. The great road beckons even as we speak. I have new songs to play."

"May the road prove ever kind to one so fine as you," said Morel, and kissed his forehead lightly. "Let every ear rejoice at the coming of fair Hamlin, minstrel, warrior, and friend."

"And do wander back this way sometime," added Leek. "You can't miss my hole. It's just left of the bok choy."

"I will indeed," said Hamlin, "for even one who wanders must have a place called home. And if I may be bold, I might say that home is here."

"Why, I'll make up the guest room straightaway," said Leek, smiling, "with fresh sheets, towels, and all."

"We have an accord," said Hamlin as he strode into the night. "Fare thee well, great givers of luck, until we meet again."

Leek and Morel watched him go and crest the rise of a hill. Hamlin turned to wave, just once, and with that, the mouse was gone. Leek sighed, but not in sadness, and turned to the she-rabbit pressed close against his side.

"Well," said Leek, "what do we do now?"

Morel took Leek's small paw. And leading him toward the garden, to the hole where they would live, she leaned in close, in a way that made his whiskers twitch, and whispered.

"Multiply."

ACKNOWLEDGMENTS

Infinite gratitude to my editor, David Linker, a man of grace and candor. Heartfelt thanks to Russell Binder, Darren Trattner, Keya Khayatian, and Julia Sachs, who deftly handle all the grown-up stuff I find so confusing. I owe untold pints at the Phoenix to my coconspirator, Brian Taylor, whose imagination far surpasses mine. Cedric Nicolas-Troyan gets an epic bear hug for teaching me the value of an unsolicited note. And Mark Osborne and Jinko Gotoh, you're the wiser, elder siblings I've always wanted. For what it's worth, I am your brother.

As for Vaughn Eugene Wascovich, the Chicago and Indiana contingents, and my extended Kenyon family, you guys prove the truth of this mythology. Because however unlucky I've felt in my life, my rabbit's always countered with magical friends.

—AK